Anything You Can Do

Marianne Stephens

Anything You Can Do

Marianne Stephens

This is a work of fiction. Names, characters, places, and incidents are products of the author's imagination or are used fictitiously and are not to be construed as real. Any resemblance to actual events, locales, organizations, or persons, living or dead, is entirely coincidental.

Copyright© 2012   Marianne Stephens

ISBN: 978-1-77101-058-0

All rights reserved. No part of this book may be used or reproduced electronically or in print without written permission, except in the case of brief quotations embodied in reviews.

Breathless Press
www.breathlesspress.com

I'd like to dedicate this book to those who've been supportive of my writing career: my family, my friends, and especially my husband, Steve. Thanks also to Justyn Perry and Barb Wilson for their hard work.

Chapter One

"Shit. Another message from that Minetti woman." Jeffrey Ryan, CEO of Ryan Industries, closed his e-mail file and shoved his chair away from his desk. Glenn in Accounting and Finance had just forwarded the latest message. Jeff closed his eyes and massaged his temples.

"Nice business term." Maggie Williams, his longtime secretary and close family friend, cleared her throat from her position in the open doorway.

Jeff dropped his hands, heaved a deep sigh, and opened his eyes. "Why the hell doesn't she stop e-mailing us?"

"Oh, I don't know. Maybe because you never authorized an actual response?" Sarcasm dripped from her retort.

"Aunt Mags, I leave this stuff up to Glenn and the planning department. If they think it's a good idea, they'll tell me."

"Might be better for you to send a definite answer." The deep crow's feet around her blue eyes crinkled as she gave Jeff a narrow-eyed look.

Jeff shook his head before answering. "You do it. Make it sound like a reasonable rejection. I'm too busy."

"Doing what? Playing online poker? Ordering Royals tickets?"

Jeff let out a loud whoosh of air and plopped his head back on his chair. "It's better than running to the casinos all the time. This way, I don't lose money. I'm just honing my skills. And," he pointed a finger at her, "I'm a big Royals fan."

The older, impeccably dressed woman gave him the same type of lecture-coming look his own mother often aimed in his direction. "You have plenty of time to give her a straight answer, even if you're not interested. But keep in mind that we may encounter some negative publicity if it gets out that Ryan Industries refuses to help a daycare center, especially one your employees use."

"You and I both know that this company decided years ago not to get involved in having a daycare facility. Dad and the board didn't consider it cost-efficient."

Maggie huffed as she approached Jeff's desk. "They're all old men who don't understand how hard it is for working mothers and single-parent families. What's your excuse?"

"Since I don't have any experience in that matter—and I'm not looking—all I can go on is what the board decided. I'm running a business. She's running a business. I take care of my company. Let her take care of hers."

Jeff recognized the disappointed-parent look Maggie gave him. She and his mother had mastered all the maternal stares. Hell, he figured they'd practiced together.

"And there sits the core of the problem." Her sermon continued in a targeted direction. "Go get married, have a family, and let me run this place. We both know I do all the work around here anyway."

Throwing his hand across his heart, he pleaded, "Aunt Mags, please. Stop talking to my mother every day. Devising devious schemes to end my bachelor days won't work. You women are all out to get me." He pointed at his computer screen. "Even Minetti."

"Your mother and I are only trying to help you find the right woman." Maggie sniffed and pursed her lips.

His laughter filled the room, and he sat up in his chair. "Help me?" he uttered as thoughts of their last attempt at matchmaking paraded through his head. "Remember the last time you two tried that? Lucky for me I found out Laura was only interested in money. Not to mention she had warrants out for her arrest in three states. Your *help* almost got me involved with an embezzler."

Maggie lowered her eyes, and a hint of redness crept up her cheeks. "Well, yes. That didn't work out like we'd hoped, but we know lots of other eligible women without records."

Jeff held up his hand. "No thanks. I'll do my own shopping. And, chasing. And I'll decide when I've found the right woman."

His affair with Laura had proved to be an embarrassment he didn't want to repeat. Casual dating and sex he could handle. Anything more had to be avoided.

Maggie placed her hands on her hips. "Your mother and I aren't getting any younger. Maybe you can speed up the pace a bit."

"Report what I just said back to Mom. I've already told her a million times, but maybe she'll listen to you." Hunching over his desk, Jeff scanned some folders and hoped the subject of their conversation would disappear.

"Find the right woman and make us happy. We desperately want to enjoy the few precious years we have left spoiling your children."

Once again, Jeff laughed as he stared at Maggie. "With my luck, you two will be pushing me around in a wheelchair in my nursing home. You and Mom need to find a new hobby. Forget trying to marry me off. Can we get back to work?"

"All right, all right. And, about Minetti." Maggie pointed a red, polished fingernail in his direction. "You can tell her yourself why you've been avoiding her requests. She's on her way over here as we speak."

Jeff wrinkled his brow and ran a hand through his dark hair as he focused on her last sentence. "She's coming here?"

Maggie threw up her arms in a sign of frustration. "Isn't that what I just said? Really, Jeffrey. You need to pay more attention."

"Why a personal visit?"

"My guess would be that she's tired of playing e-mail tag with Ryan Industries and wants to meet you face to face."

Jeff's mind whirled as he tried to find an excuse not to be available, but he couldn't come up with one. "Find me an emergency meeting to go to."

Hands back on her hips in a no-nonsense pose, Maggie responded in a clipped tone, "I will not." She pointed at him again. "Lying for you isn't in my job description."

A tinge of guilt hit Jeff as he realized trying to skip out of meeting Minetti went against his professional attitude. Why had he put off answering the owner of "Ryan's Rugrats"?

His company routinely donated to charitable organizations. Had he avoided her messages because she'd sent so many? He couldn't avoid seeing the daycare building every morning upon entering his building. Had he been slightly irritated at her for using his company's name?

Regardless, he knew the ethical importance of meeting with people, especially those asking for financial help. He glanced down at his desk, unable to look Maggie in the eye.

"You told me to schedule all your appointments and not worry you about them," Maggie continued. "Didn't you check today's appointment list? I left it on your desk. Do you want to take over my job as secretary now?"

With a shrug of resignation, Jeff looked at Maggie and gave her a false smile. "You're right. Sorry. I didn't check the list, and no, I don't want your job. You and Mom would have more time to try interfering in my life if I fired you. At least here I can keep you busy with work."

He swung his chair around to face the window as he tried to formulate a polite but unmistakable rejection, one Minetti would receive and accept. Maybe then she'd leave him alone. "When's Minetti coming?"

"I'm here, Mr. Ryan. Am I too early?"

Surprise hit him as he quickly revolved his chair to face the doorway. The nemesis he'd envisioned transformed into a beautiful young woman staring at him with sky-blue eyes surrounded by a thick fringe of lashes. Rosy full lips curved up at the corners of her mouth.

Jeff gazed at the gorgeous woman with the dazzling smile and just a hint of a blush staining her cheeks. Her penetrating eyes could totally entrance a man and cause all sane thoughts to disappear into thin air.

She was around his age and a few inches short of his six-foot height. Stunning auburn-colored hair that reached to her shoulders shone brightly in the glow provided by the overhead lights. His gaze wandered lower as he scrutinized her enticing figure, not altogether hidden by her demure dark blue suit.

Standing as a matter of instinct, Jeff geared his thoughts to remember he'd have to remain on guard. This temptress, though gorgeous, wanted something from him.

Maggie made a few tsk sounds as she broke the silence surrounding them. "Ms. Minetti, you're right on time. Please come in, and I'll leave you two alone." She pivoted to exit the room but turned back quickly to ask, "Or do I need to stay?"

Jeff aimed an "I wish I could fire you, but I need you and my mother would kill me" look at his secretary. "Thank you, but we'll be fine." He glanced at Minetti and then yelled to Maggie's retreating back, "Hold my calls, please."

Ms. Minetti stepped into the room so Maggie could pass through the doorway. Jeff noticed no wedding ring adorned her finger, and for a brief moment he wondered if she had a boyfriend. The desire to know her better planted itself firmly in his head. He watched as she sashayed her well-proportioned hips into his office.

Convinced he'd spent too much time staring at the beautiful vision and her apparent cool, calm looks, Jeff sought to utter something meaningful. When his brain finally kicked into gear, he offered a courteous invitation. "Please come in and sit down."

Allison Minetti scrutinized the man before her as she tugged at the bottom of her double-breasted jacket. She'd fastened all the buttons, assuming a prim and proper look fit the occasion. His obvious once-over and deep brown-eyed stare made her wonder if her skirt might be too short or if her choice of business attire was all wrong.

"Thank you." Keeping her voice even, she hoped the butterflies dancing in her stomach stayed hidden.

The head of Ryan Industries lowered himself into his leather seat. One of his hands raked through his dark curls, and her fingers coiled gently as she itched to push a few errant strands back into place.

Jeffrey Ryan's chiseled jaw hinted at stern but pleasant facial features when he smiled. A form-fitted crisp white shirt, accented by a striking silk blue tie, covered his broad chest. Handsome, sexy, everything she'd been warned to expect.

Even though she didn't work for his company, Allison had heard enough stories about Randy Ryan to fuel her curiosity. She'd caught snatches of gossip about his playboy lifestyle. Last year, he'd been a handsome candidate on Kansas City's "Most Eligible Bachelors" list.

Allison stiffened her spine and remembered her mission. She needed to convince him Ryan Industry's partnership would be vital in initiating the well-planned changes necessary for her daycare center's survival. Here was her chance to pitch her case for funding to improve Ryan's Rugrats.

The center needed financial help. All her clients worked for his company. She'd accommodated his employees as much as she could, but the center would close if changes weren't forthcoming. Surely he would listen and agree.

Allison watched as if mesmerized when he tilted back in his chair and rocked it in slow steady movements resulting in tiny squeaking noises. A slight hint of a grin appeared on his face. His fingertips met and tapped out an annoying soundless rhythm.

"Ms. Minetti—"

"I'd prefer Miss."

He stopped rocking. "Miss Minetti, I'm confused about something. One of your e-mails stated you have over twenty years of experience running daycare facilities." He gave her a very thorough once over again, causing a wave of heat to streak through her body. "You don't appear to be old enough for that."

Allison shifted uncomfortably in her seat. "I believe you're referring to the first group of e-mails. They were from my aunt, Abigail Minetti, who opened the daycare. I replaced her four months ago."

"That explains my confusion." An engaging smile probably meant to disarm her covered his face. Charm oozed in his tone and from his body language, lulling Allison into an all-too-comfortable position.

"I guess it does." An involuntary smile formed before sanity returned. The image of Ryan's Rugrats flashed through her head. "I received another generic response from Ryan Industries earlier this week, so I decided I'd come and see whether we could negotiate some type of partnership and funding for the center."

"I—I'll need to review your requests."

Allison nibbled on her bottom lip before speaking. "This has been going on for quite some time. I really hoped to settle this today."

"Oh. Uh, give me a minute."

Jeff turned his attention to his computer and typed on his keyboard. "Your e-mail file is here somewhere." He looked up at her. "Quite honestly, I haven't had the opportunity to read through them all. I just got back from a business trip."

"Maybe I should make another appointment for Monday and give you a chance to review everything. I'll speak to your secretary and set one up. Thank you." She rose from her seat and began to walk away.

"I won't be in the office Monday."

She turned to face him, swinging her curly hair in the process. "Okay. I'll try for Tuesday then."

"That won't work either."

Allison couldn't stop a slight frown from appearing on her face. "Are we at some type of standstill, Randy Ry—I mean, Mr. Ryan?"

Jeff winced at her almost-choice of words. "No. Really. I—"

Maggie opened the door and poked her head into the room. "Sorry to interrupt, but you have a luncheon engagement in thirty minutes. Should I have the car brought around to the front?"

Relieved at Maggie's timing, Allison blessed the opportunity to change the subject and hide her partial Randy Ryan slip.

Jeff answered, "Right. I almost forgot about that." He aimed a winning smile at Allison and in a smooth tone asked, "Miss Minetti, won't you join me for lunch?"

The invitation startled her, but Allison realized she could use the outing to pitch her request. Plus, the rumbling in her stomach reminded her she'd skipped breakfast in her rush to get to work.

Jeff Ryan appealed to her in an inherent woman-needs-to-chase-sexy-man type of way. Hell. The man was handsome and loaded with sex appeal. She itched to find out what made his nickname the fountain of whispered gossip. This was no time to be shy.

"Would I be interrupting your luncheon meeting?"

He turned to Maggie and asked, "Isn't the Archbishop meeting me there?"

"Yes."

Jeff gave Allison a quick grin and offered, "He's an old family friend and helps organize all the charitable events we sponsor. He won't mind you coming along."

"Are you sure? I don't want to impose."

"No problem. Would you wait out there with Mrs. Williams for a few minutes? I have some things to finish before we leave."

"Certainly." Allison ambled out of the room and closed the door. "Mrs. Williams—"

"It's Maggie." The older woman's smile held a warm greeting.

"I'm Allison."

Maggie pointed a finger in Allison's direction. "Honey, don't let him bulldoze you when you speak to him. Tell him up front what you want and why."

"The center desperately needs financial help, or it'll close. I knew my rent would be going up, but I just found out it will almost double next month when I have to sign a new lease. I had hoped to expand to the empty building next door and do some remodeling so I can care for more kids. Now I can't afford any of it." Her stomach tightened at the thought.

Maggie reached over and patted Allison's hand. "Now don't you worry. He's a tiger at business. We've got five major complexes to handle and more computer design and programming work than Kansas City can throw our way." She winked and continued, "Deep down inside he's an old softie. Keep that in mind."

A tiger? Maybe he used that style with women and that's what kept the gossip about him going strong. An old softie? Ryan Industries was one of the major benefactors for many charities. She prayed that translated into an approachable Jeff, one open-minded to new ideas.

Jeff?

Hormones and anxiety had to be behind her lack of mind control in using his first name. Allison sought to keep fantasy at bay and reality front and center in her brain.

"Time to go. See you later, Mrs. Williams."

Jeff's sudden appearance made Allison jump. She offered a quick wave to Maggie before walking through the door he held open.

At the elevator, Jeff pushed the down button. When the doors opened, he stepped aside and gestured for Allison to step into the antiquated car.

Should she try to stir up a conversation? Or stare at the panel of floor numbers as they lit up? Maybe she could just scan the interior as if interested in every decorating detail.

Jeff—her mind now hell-bent on calling him that—broke through her nervous brain ramblings and ended the silence.

"I guess it'll go faster if one of us pushes number one." He laughed.

"Sure. Go ahead." *Nine floors to go. This will take forever.* Allison remained standing in place and rooted to the ground in front of the button panel.

His hand brushed against hers as he sought to select their floor destination button. "Pardon me."

The light touch of his hand tingled along her skin. Some whispered quotes about his attributes came to mind. What had Helen said? Something to do with his muscled biceps? The warm and gentle stroke of his hand?

Jeff interrupted her foray into daydreaming. He dug through a pocket and pulled out a slip of paper. "Says here we're going to the Rainbow Towers Restaurant. Ever been there?"

"No."

He tilted his head and stared at her through narrowed eyes. "Why all the e-mails? What? Every week? Every other week?"

"It wasn't that often."

"Seems like that to me." He shrugged.

Her mouth remained open and void of sound before her brain decided to form coherent sentences. "Maybe this isn't such a good idea. Why don't I get out, go back to your office, and reschedule an appointment with Maggie? That'll give you a chance to review the file you have on Ryan's Rugrats."

She tipped forward and reached out to the panel where she repeatedly jammed the button for the next floor. Jeff unsettled her, and she needed to rethink her plan of action. But the wonderful scent of his cologne filled the air and urged her to relax while she inhaled deeply. Her next meeting with him wouldn't include the too-close setting, controlling her mind and speech, they now shared.

"Please come for lunch." Jeff's hand landed on her outstretched one.

"I think it's best if I get off," she said.

His minimal physical contact with her initiated a catch in her breath, and her heart skipped a beat. It was time to cut her losses before she unleashed any additional unnerved reactions. She eased her hand from his and resumed poking the button. When she noticed they'd passed the floor, she pressed some of the other buttons.

"I think we may have a problem." Jeff maneuvered closer to the panel and examined the buttons. "The lights are going on, but we're not stopping."

Her beautiful eyes widened and held his attention as she asked, "Can you fix it, Mr. Ryan?"

Jeff noted her use of his proper name, unlike her almost use of his nickname in his office. At that time, her pink blush had darkened and made her more adorable.

Shit. His nickname, the one bandied around town that he'd tried to ignore and prove false, haunted him no matter how hard he tried to distance himself from it.

Discreet attempts to keep his personal life inconspicuous somehow always failed. Exaggerated renditions as to whom he dated and all the particulars filtered through the ranks of his company and the general community on a routine basis.

Allison was charming and quickly captivated his attention. Before he could squelch the idea that popped into his head, he'd blurted out an invitation to lunch. He didn't know what had happened.

Forcing his brain to concentrate on their elevator situation instead of daydreaming, he answered, "It may just be a temporary glitch. I'm sure it'll stop at the next floor."

The sound of screeching wires filled the air. The elevator jolted to a complete stop.

Chapter Two

As the elevator jerked, one of Jeff's arms curved around Allison while the other braced against the wall to steady them. Heat cascaded throughout her body as he tightened his grip and plastered her to him like a second skin. The lights almost dimmed enough to send them into complete darkness.

"Are you all right?" He freed her from his hold, stepped to the side, and pressed the red emergency button. "Cell phones don't work in here, so let's hope someone hears the alarm."

Allison remembered to breathe again and shivered at the sudden loss of warmth his nearness had created. The overwhelming sensation of comfort had dissipated when he'd moved away. Panic settled in, and she pounded on the door, yelling for help.

"Can't you get it going again?" Although she fought for control, even she could hear a desperate tone creeping into her voice. Remaining in his company after being held in his arms required thoughts of rescue and not how much she desired another embrace.

A frown shadowed by the miniscule lighting covered his face. "Not from here. I pressed the emergency button."

"Hello down there! Everyone okay?" A voice from floors above broke into their discussion.

"We're fine! What happened?" Jeff asked.

"It's Robert, Mr. Ryan. The electrical box fried, and the backup generator got jammed, too. Don't know why, but we'll get you out as soon as we can. Just sit tight."

"Thanks," Jeff shouted.

"I have to get out of here." Allison spoke the words rampaging through her head. Being so near Jeff sparked every sensual nerve in her body.

He blinked and asked, "You're not claustrophobic, are you?"

She shook her head. "No. I'm, uh, just wondering how long we'll be stuck in here." Allison surveyed their small confining space and wished for a fast escape.

"Robert's working on it. So, we'll just have to relax."

Relax? Jeff was too close. The only things she craved to do involved running her hands through his hair, melding her body against his again, and checking out some of the rumors about him. Maybe if she talked about the center, her wandering thoughts and itching hands would behave.

She took a deep breath and then blurted out, "Ryan's Rugrats needs funding, or it'll close. The rent's going to increase, and I've sent every imaginable outline, estimate, and financial plan your company has requested. Why all the stalling? Do I need to stand on my head or beg?"

Jeff's chestnut-colored eyes pierced into her. "You don't waste time with pleasantries. Do you mind if I sit down?" Not waiting for her response, he slid out of his suit jacket and spread it on the floor. "Care to join me? We may be here a while."

Crap. Maybe she'd come on too strong. Her high heels pinched her feet, adding to her frustration. "No. I'll just take off my shoes and stand here."

"Fine. Look. I really need time to review everything. I can't just rush into this."

She sighed and folded her arms across her body. "This has been going on for months. Maybe you should come to the center and see for yourself."

"What? Watch you babysit kids?"

Allison tried to remain calm. "Jeff, we do not babysit kids. We provide education and care. There's a difference."

He sat down, leaned back against a wall, and smirked. "How hard can that be?"

"Oh? I bet you couldn't do it without seeing why we need improvements." An idea popped into her head. Smug with confidence, Allison issued her challenge. "I dare you to."

Jeff's eyes widened. "Me? Babysit kids? Why would I?"

Wheels churned in her head as she sought out a way to solidify her dare into a plan. "Tell you what. If you can spend one week with me at the center, survive, and not see the need for partnership funding, I'll stop sending requests."

"I don't have time for that."

"Afraid you'd lose?"

Jeff raised an eyebrow and placed both hands behind his head. "What do you get if you win?"

"Your promise to honestly look into my financial partnership request."

"That's it? No guarantee of partnership with Ryan's Rugrats or X-amount of money?"

She shook her head. "Nope. Just your promise to consider my business growth plan."

"Sounds like I get the better end of this. I win, and you stop e-mailing me."

Allison placed her hands on her hips. "When you lose, I let your conscience be your guide. And," she decided to add an additional condition to their dare, "one more thing, Jeff. You get to tell me the story of your life. That should amuse me while you write out a check to Ryan's Rugrats."

A devilish grin covered Jeff's face. "I want to add a consequence for you if I win."

"Why? Getting me to stop sending requests isn't enough?"

"You added something extra, so I should also be able to. If I win, you spend a weekend with me."

Allison directed a glare at him. She didn't care if he couldn't sense the full effect in their darkened confines. "You better clarify that before I get the wrong impression."

"I mean as a friend, nothing else. Downtown hotel, separate rooms. Keep me company. We can act like visitors and see the sights. That's all."

She relaxed her stance. "That I can do. But since I won't lose, you'll be spending the weekend alone."

"We'll see about that. And just to prove my good faith in all this, I'll bore you with some of my life story right now." He patted a spot next to him. "Have a seat. You have to be tired standing there. Since you've already found yourself comfortable enough to use my first name, do you mind if I drop the Miss Minetti formality and call you Allison?"

Energy drained from her body as the warm air in the elevator melted her stamina. She unbuttoned her jacket, thankful for the tank top she'd worn underneath it. "First names are fine with me."

After angling her body next to his, she tried to relax. The scent of his sweet-smelling mouthwash enticed her senses. The skin on her face prickled wherever his breath touched. Regardless of her attempts to control her body, it reacted instinctively to Jeff's presence. The rhythm of her breathing remained elevated, and her heart pounded against her chest.

Damn. What a time for her hormones to go into overdrive. "Is it getting hot in here?" She fanned her face with her hand. At twenty-nine, she was too young for hot flashes. Jeffrey Ryan had made her temperature soar.

Man, she smelled wonderful. He breathed in a heady mix of honey and roses. His beautiful, sexy, trapped companion was a thorn in his side with all her e-mails, but he'd forever associate the sweet-smelling scents with the name Allison.

She had teased him into having sexual fantasies from the moment he'd first seen her alluring feminine frame grace the doorway of his office. He'd noticed all her curves from the swell of her breasts as they snuggled forward against the silky material of her jacket to the straight seams of her skirt molded to her hips.

Her body cried out for male caresses and offered the promise of pleasant retribution to the man who obliged. Holding her in his arms for a few moments when the elevator jerked and stopped had left his body charged and agreeable to any intimate position Allison wished. Jeff wanted nothing more than to have a frenzied erotic fling with her to satisfy his hunger and desire. Thoughts of satisfying his sexual need for her fired up his already male reaction. His arousal stretched against his zipper, aching for a caress.

Allison snatched some tissues from her purse and wiped her face and neck. "Want one? I have plenty."

Jeff stuffed his hand in his jacket pocket and removed a handkerchief. "No thanks. I've got this."

He wiped at the sweat beading on his forehead. An involuntary chuckle escaped as he recalled how she'd manipulated him into accepting her dare. What the hell, he could do it. He ran a major company. How hard could it be to watch some kids?

Allison pulled her legs closer to her body and crossed her arms in front of her as if to ward off a marauding enemy. "Is it getting hotter?"

Lady, it sure is. "The air's probably not filtering right."

She clutched her curly hair and raised it off her neck. "I wish I'd brought a clip."

"What about my tie? I know it's bulky, but maybe it'll give you some relief."

"Won't that ruin it? I mean, if I knot it?"

"Not a problem." He took off his tie and handed it to her.

Allison took it and wound it around her dark hair. After a few seconds, she asked, "Can you help me? I can't get the knot tight enough and hold up my hair at the same time."

"Sure." Jeff slipped his hands across the back of her neck and pulled the two tie ends into a knot. He leaned in and inhaled her scent.

"Thanks."

Allison concentrated on breathing in a normal pattern to calm herself. While they sat all too close to each on the elevator's floor, Jeff told some amusing stories.

"I had a normal childhood, given we may have been in a higher income bracket than most. I'm a sports nut, always have been and still am. I played football in high school and college. Had to do something to catch the girls' attention. I even have the proverbial football injury to verify my stories." He stretched his arms and rubbed his left leg.

Allison replied mockingly, "Uh-huh. Get any studying done?"

"Hello down there! Shouldn't be too much longer!" the muted voice from above shouted words of encouragement.

"Please hurry! It's hot down here!" Allison yelled back.

While searching for a more comfortable position, she bumped into Jeff's thigh with her knee. She quickly shifted her position and tucked her legs nearer to her body. Warm air blanketed her thighs as her skirt hiked up with the movement.

"To finish my college story, I did more than just date. I got a master's degree in business and here I am now, using all those wonderful skills I learned." He looked around them. "Too bad fixing elevators wasn't in one of my courses." He rolled up his shirt sleeves revealing muscled arms.

"You forgot something," she teased.

Jeff turned to stare at her. "Like what?"

"How did you get your nickname?"

Jeff exhaled a long deep breath. "Unfortunately, my dating escapades earned me the reputation of being a Romeo in college. The whole damn name thing ballooned out of control. Every time I date someone, it turns into an exaggerated affair thanks to the Randy Ryan ghost haunting my life. Does that appease your curiosity?"

"Oh, I'm sure there's a lot more to your story, but yes, I'll accept that."

"Good. Now it's my turn to ask about you."

She stretched and wiggled her shoulders as she tried to sit up straight instead of sagging against the wall. "What do you want to know?"

He rested his head against the wall. "Everything. We have plenty of time."

Chapter Three

Allison thought she'd go crazy. Being stuck in an overheated elevator within kissing distance of a sexy, charming man, made her crave to purr like a kitten. The electricity charging the air between them should've been enough to jumpstart the elevator.

As sanity warred with the fantasies marching through her brain, Allison scooted a short distance away from Jeff. She smoothed her skirt before pushing back the damp curls clinging to her forehead. Damn his kissable lips. Their closeness weakened her control and made her vulnerable.

"I wish they'd work faster." Exhaustion and the heat, coupled with embarrassment and passion, tore at her composure.

"So. One week with you and the kids. I won't be left alone with them, right?" A tinge of nervousness colored his question.

Allison laughed and then said in a nonchalant tone, "Absolutely not. I have to make sure they're taken care of in case you decide to escape."

A sly grin spread across his face. "Just checking. I wouldn't wanna whip them into shape and encroach on your territory."

A niggling doubt crossed her mind. When he'd accepted the challenge, she'd been positive he wouldn't be able to handle even one day in the daycare. Could he make it through a week?

"I've gotta stand up and stretch. Maybe the air from the vent will reach my head quicker that way." Jeff maneuvered his body into an upright position. "Hey, I think it's cooler when you stand." He offered his hand to Allison.

She grasped it, and prickles of heat raced up her arm. He gave a gentle tug and helped her up. Once standing, Allison wiggled her hand free and concentrated on yanking down her skirt. Doing something, anything, helped her forget his burning touch. "Yep, it's cooler this way." She fanned her face with her hand.

"Should we shake hands and seal our deal?" Jeff stretched out his hand to once again encase hers.

"Let me make sure I absolutely understand this. If you live through one week of daycare, all I have to do is accompany you around town for a weekend, no strings attached?"

He drew back his hand and placed it over his heart. "That's the deal and all I ask." He grinned and added in a sexy tone, "Unless you decide to change the rules."

Allison considered the realities of their agreement. Although confident she'd win, logic wormed its way into her assessment of their dare. Even if she lost, she'd be in his company. She could sneak her requests into their conversations, so it wouldn't be a total defeat.

"Hey down there! Grab onto something or hit the floor. I'm gonna start up the motor!"

With one huge grating sound, the elevator jolted and rocked into action, causing them to lose their balance. They stumbled as the car sped upward. Jeff landed in a sitting position.

Unsteady on her feet, Allison tripped and lost her footing. Jeff reached out, gripped her hips to stop her from falling backward, and pulled her down toward him. She landed with unladylike grace in his lap, renting inches of splits in her skirt seams as she straddled his body.

They grabbed onto each other, locked in an intimate embrace. Basic instincts took over. Her lips slid across his, and her hands wound into his curly hair. His tongue teased her into a frenzy of soul-searching kisses.

Jeff groaned and moved his head back to rest against the wall. "Wow. Very nice."

With her heart pounding, Allison reeled as she tried to regain her composure. His kiss left her panting for more. She missed hearing the elevator door open.

"I see you managed to occupy yourselves," a woman's voice stated.

Reality hit Allison as a rush of cool air flowed in from the opened door. She cringed with embarrassment at the woman's comment. Her seam-split skirt clung mid-thigh as her legs spread out on either side of Jeff's body. She still had her arms wrapped around his shoulders.

Jeff tilted his head past hers to peer out the open door. "Mother, this is Allison Minetti. Allison, this is my mother, Elizabeth Ryan."

Allison blinked and then stared into the face of the man she shared an intimate position with. His words carried a sense of humor. A heated flush rose up her cheeks, and she swiveled her head to face his mother. A tall, elegantly dressed woman stood next to Maggie.

The women stood gaping into the elevator along with a man in a maintenance uniform. All three had huge grins on their faces.

"Uh, hi. Nice to meet you," Allison muttered.

"Would you like us to close the door again?" Maggie asked before she burst out laughing.

"No, thank you," Jeff said.

Allison's brain kicked into gear and urged her to stand. She pushed away from him and swung one leg over his body. She got to her knees and tried to get up. Stumbling, she plopped back down into Jeff's lap.

"Oomph," Jeff said with a gasp.

Two hands grabbed under her arms and pulled her into a standing position. Full of gratitude, she turned and read the name on the uniform. "Thank you, Robert."

"Sure, miss. Now if you two will get outta here, I'll work on the panel. Not sure what set it off."

Jeff jumped up. "Allison did it."

In the midst of bending to grasp her jacket, she turned toward him and glared. "I said I was sorry."

"I'm teasing you. Forget it."

"I better leave." She held her head up high and took a step toward the opened doorway. When Jeff called her name, she pivoted to face him.

"Don't you want these?" He scooped up her heels and dangled them in front of her. "You can use my office bathroom to put yourself back together."

"Thank you, Mr. Ryan." With as much dignity as her limp countenance could muster, she rescued her shoes from his grasp and followed Maggie into the office area.

As he corralled his jacket, Jeff sensed his mother staring at him.

"Should I expect a lawsuit?"

"Nothing happened. The elevator bolted and knocked us down. End of story."

His mother raised both eyebrows. "Oh?"

"If you don't mind, I'm going to head home to shower and put on some clean clothes." Jeff shook a finger in his mother's direction. "Did you and Maggie have anything to do with this elevator breakdown? It wouldn't surprise me if you tried to play matchmakers again and figured trapping us in this damn thing would help your cause."

Elizabeth glared at him. "We had nothing to do with this. Don't take it out on me if the woman has the good sense to reject you."

"Who said anything about her rejecting me?" Jeff shrugged into his jacket.

"She didn't?"

"Hell, no. She's a great kisser and…Oh, no." He laughed and shook his head. "You're not tricking me into saying anything more."

"I'm sure I don't know what you mean. Did we interrupt something?"

Hot, frustrated, and irritated, Jeff held up a warning hand. "This conversation is over."

"All right, all right. Go home and change. You look awful." She shook her head. "You probably put that poor girl through hell."

Jeff smiled at his mother as he walked past her to head for the stairs. Ten flights of steps awaited him, but he figured reviewing his trapped elevator scenario with a beautiful, enticing woman named Allison would fill his time.

Her scent clung to his clothing and his deep inhale triggered an arousal. When they'd fallen to the elevator floor and she'd landed on top of him, nature had taken over. The thought of making love to Allison had exploded in his mind.

She'd returned his kisses with passion, something that had surprised him and probably her. Being with her for a week would be heavenly, even if he had to go through the motions of her challenge.

Jeff strolled out of the stairwell and walked to the front door of his building. Ryan's Rugrats came into view, and he let out a laugh at her thinking he couldn't handle working with her and some kids. He'd do his week and hope to have one hell of a weekend with Allison. If their elevator kissing was an indication of her willingness for exploring sexual encounters with him, he was more than ready to satisfy some lusty fantasies taking form in his mind.

"Maggie, would you do me a favor? Please call the center and tell them I'll be late getting back." Allison tossed the comment over her shoulder as she entered Jeff's private bathroom. Once inside, she surveyed her reflection in the mirror and rolled her eyes. She looked like something a cat repeatedly dragged in without mercy.

Her hair, some of it still held in a Jeff-tied ponytail, displayed all the shine and beauty of a dull, dusty window. Mostly limp, some strands hugged her face as others just hung down. The little makeup she'd worn had evaporated. Her lips, void of lipstick, appeared full and ripe, as if someone had been busy doing his damnedest to kiss the hell out of them. Placing a finger on her upper lip, Allison traced a full circle.

With a desire to satisfy her lust first and contend with sanity later, she'd followed his lead with full wanton approval and a hunger of her own.

Allison checked the torn seams in her skirt and tucked her tank top into her waistband. She stared into the mirror again and witnessed a rosy blush staining her cheeks at the thought of intimate contact and kisses.

Removing Jeff's silk tie from her hair, she cringed at the crinkly marks left where it had been knotted. Vowing to get it cleaned for him, she splashed cold water on her face, used a towel to dry it, draped her hair behind her ears, and opened the door.

Opposite the doorway sat Elizabeth Ryan, major stockholder and board member of the company. Pillar of society. The mother of the man whose body Allison couldn't deny wanting. Shaking herself into reality, Allison strode into the room before looking at her feet. The ones without shoes on.

"Excuse me, Mrs. Ryan. I'll just go back in there and put on my shoes. I'll be out of here in a minute."

"Stop right there. Come here and sit down."

Allison grabbed her shoes and walked to an empty seat near Elizabeth. Tired from her elevator ordeal, she dropped into the chair without any semblance of grace. The older woman's eyes sparkled as her mouth curled up at the corners. Allison noted she had the same warm brown eyes and wavy hair as Jeff.

Allison bent over to cram her feet into her heels before speaking. "Mrs. Ryan, I know what it looked like when that door opened. But, nothing happened."

Elizabeth's eyes narrowed. "Not even a kiss?"

Heat flamed Allison's cheeks. "Uh, well, we did kiss. But nothing else."

The other woman laughed. "Oh, Allison. It's really none of my business." She sighed. "Men. Jeffrey can be so aggravating at times. I either want to hug him or kill him. The latter appeals when he acts up."

Maggie strolled into the room. "I brought you a cold drink."

Allison guzzled the icy drink and watched the in-depth whispering bantered between the two older ladies. The jarring ring of Jeff's telephone startled all of them.

Maggie answered it. With a sly smile on her face, she held out the phone to Allison. "It's for you, dear."

Assuming it was someone from the center, Allison took the phone and said, "This is Allison."

"It's Jeff."

"Why are you calling me here?" she replied, trying to keep the embarrassment welling inside her from coloring her tone.

"I figured you'd still be there."

"Listen here, Randy Ryan—" Cringing and spinning around, Allison observed both Maggie and Elizabeth choking back what had to be laughter desperate to escape from their lips. "I mean, Mr. Ryan. What do you want?"

"I want you to know that I'm planning to clear my calendar for next week so I can spend time with you and the little ones."

"Good. I'll just be there to make sure you don't run screaming from the center and leave the kids alone."

Allison's smugness escalated as she listened to the two women in the room roar with laughter.

"Oh, I'll do just fine. Pack your suitcase."

"I have no plans to pack a suitcase. You'll never finish your week," she quipped with confidence.

"Okay with me. Come with the clothes on your back. I'll offer my T-shirt for you to sleep in."

Allison remained speechless for a few seconds. Wear his shirt? Sleep naked in his clothes? In a hotel room? No sex?

Of course there won't be sex, she chided herself.

"I'll see you bright and early on Monday. Rest up this weekend. You'll need it," Allison said.

"You too. You'll need all your strength for next weekend. Would you please put Maggie on the phone?"

Dismissed, she dangled the receiver in her hand and nodded in Maggie's direction. "He wants to speak to you."

Allison left the building and quickly got in her car for her short ride home. Thoughts of Jeff and their kiss floated through her mind, and she cautioned herself not to put too much emphasis on what had happened. Chances were close to zero that without being trapped in the elevator none of their intimate contact would ever have happened.

She parked in her apartment lot and got out. Allison immediately headed for her bedroom where she collapsed on the bed, relieved to be alone. Her crazy day had started out so innocently with her determination, pride, and sex drive positively in their correct places and under control.

Her meeting plan of action had taken too many detours after she'd so carefully organized every detail: go to the main office, confront Mr. Ryan, make him see the absolute need to become an investment partner with the center, impress him with all the details, be business-like, and hold an intelligent conversation.

Instead, Allison's brain had registered "fight and win him over." Her heart melted and pumped twenty times faster than usual, signaling a breach in her no-man-now defenses.

She recalled how his eyes had penetrated her soul. Her head told her to be sensible, but her body cried out for satisfaction, driven to end the attraction building inside.

Allison clutched her pillow and hugged it to her body. Hell, he probably just did what came naturally. He was there, and she was sitting in his lap. They were stuck, so he reached out to grab what was handy. Most likely, he'd never give her the time of day except in this one unusual circumstance.

"Too damn bad," she grumbled into her pillow.

She got up and began removing her clothes. A warm shower would help wash away the remnants of their heated scene. When she finally stepped into the spray, Allison willed her head to think along the lines of something more practical. The daycare needed her to perform miracles.

Jeff rummaged through his discarded clothes after showering. The suit he'd worn in the elevator disaster lay in a heap on his bedroom floor and had to be dry-cleaned. His shirt, underwear, and socks were thrown into a laundry bag.

The air chilled his moist skin as he bent over his suit jacket. One hand held the towel draped around his waist in place, while the other removed items from his coat pockets.

Had she gone home and showered as he had, washing away any traces of their elevator adventure? He'd love to see her naked and wet in a shower with him. He vowed to win their bet and spend the weekend with her.

The bumping and jostling of their crazy elevator adventure had done a number on his muscles. At thirty-three, he wasn't in the same physically fit state he'd been in when he'd played college football. Jeff noted that apparently more time at the gym would be needed, although he wouldn't have time to work in some sessions until after his week in daycare and his weekend with Allison.

What if she already had plans? He frowned. For some reason, he didn't like the idea that she might spend weekends with other men. Shit. Maybe some of his brain cells had fried in the elevator. Why should he care about her sex life? He had no reason to be jealous.

Jealous? Randy Ryan, the epitome of carefree bachelorhood? After spending a week with her, he'd get her out of his system. Another woman to wine and dine, no attachments or commitments.

Oh, he'd get through the daycare nonsense without a hitch, regardless of how she doubted him. Then it would be his turn to get what he wanted. Smug with male logic at his ability to handle anything, Jeff welcomed his upcoming challenge. After all, he loved kids. One day he hoped to find the right woman and have some of his own. Monday with Ryan's Rugrats would be a piece of cake.

Chapter Four

"It's Sunday. What are you doing here?" Allison aimed her question at Jeff, who'd startled her by waltzing into the daycare center's open doorway.

"I was working in my office and noticed a car in your parking lot. I thought I'd check it out. What are you doing here? Trying to sabotage things for me before I take charge tomorrow?"

Allison stood up, pushing herself away from the art supply corner, and dusted off her hands. "No, of course not. I have no need to do anything. You'll do that to yourself. I came in to make up some of the time I lost during our elevator disaster."

Jeff ran the fingers of one hand along a counter-top. "Not all of it was so bad," he commented suggestively.

"Bad enough." Allison tried to hide her embarrassment behind an I-really-don't-know-what-you-mean-by-that look.

"I've cleared my schedule, so I'm ready for tomorrow. I hope you're ready for our weekend." He rocked back and forth on his heels.

"I'm not worried. And, I've already called all the parents to let them know you'll be helping this week." Allison said. "By the way, how's your mother?"

With a lopsided smirk, Jeff replied, "She blames me for not having the elevator fixed years ago."

"Uh, about what happened yesterday?" She couldn't meet his gaze. "I was suffering from heatstroke and didn't know what I was doing."

She fidgeted with toys in the animal corner to keep her mind focused anywhere other than on Jeff's aftershave wafting through the air as it tried to draw her under his spell. Not looking up at him made no difference. Prickles of heat danced up her body at his nearness.

"So, you don't make it a habit of kissing every man you get trapped in an elevator with? It's an interesting pick-up move, though."

"Actually, it's you who kissed me. Maybe it's part of Randy Ryan's standard moves. As for me, you're the only man I've kissed in an elevator. And hopefully the last." Allison seized a stuffed elephant and lobbed it at his head.

Jeff caught it and tucked it under his arm. "Nope. I can honestly say I've never kissed a beautiful woman in an elevator before." He smiled and continued in a sexy drawl, "You're my first."

Allison spun around, surveying the room. "I'm desperately searching for something harder and heavier to throw at you. Don't get me riled, Mr. Ryan."

Sounds of laughter followed her as she stalked off and headed for the kitchen area.

"So, boss, do I bring a lunch? Or do we send out for food? I need to know some of the particulars before showing up tomorrow."

While opening and slamming shut various cabinet doors, Allison gave a hasty reply. "The kids bring their food. The kitchen's kinda small and needs newer appliances as you can see. You can bring your lunch or have it delivered, whatever you want. Caviar, lobster, wine—"

"Funny. Real funny. Think that's what I do all day? Eat expensive food on company time?"

"No," she sniffed. "I just assumed you'd want to order from your favorite restaurants and have them cater your meals."

"You're determined to give me a hard time. How about easing up a little? You did do a lap dance on me." He wiggled his eyebrows at her.

She crashed a pot down on the stove-top. "I'll ease up if you will. Look, we'll be working pretty close here with the kids. No more talk about Friday, okay? I'll do my job, and you do yours."

Hopping up on the counter next to her, Jeff gave Allison a boyish grin that melted her heart and curled her toes. Damn him.

"Deal. No more about Friday. Just start thinking about what to bring this weekend. I've got big plans for us."

Hands on her hips, Allison laughed. "Oh, right. I forgot your fantasy plans. Sure, I'll be thinking about that all week, up until you run screaming from here and admit defeat."

"You don't know me very well, Miss Minetti. I don't give up without a fierce fight." He jumped down and pointed a finger at her. "See you ringside tomorrow."

After a wink and quick turn, he strolled out of the room. Allison squelched the split-second urge bouncing through her brain that told her to run after him.

Bright and early in the morning, Allison gave a careful evaluation of his outfit as Jeff ambled his way into the daycare center. She stifled the laughter threatening to escape. Clueless to daycare chaos, the man had chosen to wear his business attire. He causally tossed his jacket onto a chair.

"Good morning, Mr. Jeff. That's what the kids will call you."

"Morning. Where is everyone?"

This will be fun, Allison thought as she checked her watch. "Alex and Robert will be here any minute. Susan comes in next, followed by the Mercer twins, Rina and Tina. Today's Monday, so Heather, Marcus, Connor, Joel, and Jesse will be here from eight to twelve, then Austen, Tanner, Rachel, Greg, and Debbie come from twelve to five. And that's just today's schedule."

With a frown Jeff asked, "Don't you have the same kids every day? Sounds pretty complicated."

"Well," she continued, "that's because of shift work, job-sharing, and part-timers. The schedule has to adjust to the needs of the parents. You'd understand more if you read my e-mails."

"Sure. Fine. Whatever. Are there name tags or something?" Jeff looked around the room. "What do I do first?"

Pointing a finger to a chart hanging by the kitchen door, Allison answered, "There's everything for today. I'll make up the schedule for you each morning. I guess I really can't expect you to do that part of the job."

"How accommodating."

"That's me. Helpful to a fault. Before the kids come in, read the small print on the chart. I added some extras you'll need to know about." She shrugged her shoulders. "Other than that, you're on your own. I'll be here to help, but I've got tons of work to do."

"Wait a minute. Don't you have helpers? Surely you don't do this by yourself."

"If you'll read what I wrote out, it'll explain everything. I'd hurry up if I were you. Not much time until your rugrats come."

With a huff, Jeff walked over to the chart and began reading out loud. "Make name tags." Okay, he could do that. "Grab Tina as she arrives and seat her next to the green trash can." Huh? "Make sure Alex gets Barney before Robert, since it's Alex's turn to have him first today." Barney? "Allison? Don't the kids just come in and play? What's all this stuff about?"

Poking her head out the kitchen door, she answered, "You'll find blank name tags on that table by the door. You have maybe five minutes to write them before the first kid arrives. I suggest you do that right away. Then, just follow the schedule. Should be easy for a top executive like you." She disappeared back into the kitchen.

"Yeah. Thanks for all your help!" Jeff yelled.

"Oh, be sure to print their names. We're trying to expose them to letters."

"Sure. That makes sense." How difficult could it be to control ten kids?

A few minutes later, Jeff had completed eight name tags when three children came through the door. Wearing his Mr. Jeff label, he strolled over to greet his charges.

"Hi there. I'm Mr. Jeff, and I'll be working with you today."

Three sets of eyes peered up at him. Smiles vanished, and their mouths opened. One father and two mothers nodded to Jeff and then ushered a redheaded boy, a blonde girl, and a brown-haired boy inside. After walking their kids to the coat rack, they quickly turned and exited.

"Uh, why don't you tell me your names, and I'll give you a name tag." Jeff assumed he'd made a reasonable request. Wouldn't that get them to like him?

"No!" the redheaded boy yelled. "Stranger, stranger!"

No sooner had he done this then the other two started screaming the same thing, pointing accusing fingers in Jeff's direction.

Allison dashed out of the kitchen and raced over to the screaming preschoolers. "Hey, you guys. It's okay. This is Mr. Jeff, my special helper."

The kids became silent.

"He's here for the whole week and will do all kinds of fun stuff with you." She glanced at Jeff. "Right, Mr. Jeff?"

"Uh, sure. Fun stuff."

With a wide smile covering her face, Allison added, "Now don't forget, Mr. Jeff's in charge. You ask him anything you want. I'll be making some surprise snacks in the kitchen." Checking the clock, she added, "It's Cheryl's day to help. She should be here by ten. Let's keep our fingers crossed she makes it."

"Why wouldn't she come? Doesn't she want to get paid?" Jeff questioned as he absentmindedly placed name tags on the kids.

"Her due date's tomorrow. In fact, three of the helpers are due this month, so we're running on a tentative schedule. And they don't get paid. They volunteer since they have kids who come here. All the parents are supposed to help, but things get crazy sometimes. And, you need to switch the boys' name tags." She pivoted and hurried back to the kitchen.

"Hey! It's my turn to have Barney!"

Jeff did a one-hundred-and-eighty-degree turn as he zeroed in on the fight taking place.

"Wait a minute. I'll settle this." He jogged over to the two boys, each with a hand on the purple dinosaur and neither looking like they'd soon let go.

"It's my turn, Mr. Jeff. Make Robert let go."

Jeff pulled off the two name tags and reissued them to the correct bodies. "Sorry I mixed up your names even though your parents told me when you came in. Now, Robert, let Alex have it. I believe it's his turn today."

Robert held on tighter and shook his head. "No. And you can't make me. I didn't have him yesterday, so it's my turn."

Jeff held out his hands to the two protagonists. "Look, guys, Miss Allison said it was Alex's turn. And Robert, you didn't have Barkley yesterday because it was Sunday and nobody was here."

Two miniature males turned kid-annoyed faces up to him. Maybe they didn't like his explanation.

"It's Barney," Robert mumbled. "And I'm gonna tell my daddy on you. You're mean. He's gonna come and kick you." He dropped the toy and stalked away.

Jeff sagged and then looked at the clock. A whole five minutes had gone by. Three kids there and seven more to come. Could he leave now, admit defeat, and still get Allison?

A hand tugged at his pant's leg. "Mr. Gef? I hafta go to the bathroom." Soft baby-blue eyes looked up at him under blonde ringlet curls.

Clearing his throat, Jeff said, "Go ahead, Susan."

Starting to do a one-foot-up, one-foot-down dance, she responded with urgency in her voice, "But I don't 'member where it is."

"Oh. It's over there."

After he pointed out the right direction, Susan raced away.

Allison stepped into the room. "Mr. Jeff? Ready for the twins now? They'll be here any minute. Tina's the one who hates being here and sits by the trash can."

Her smile raised his temperature. So did watching her bend over a brooding Robert. *Nice view*, he thought as her rear end stretched the jeans covering that part of her body. He'd stay put.

"No problem."

Jeff walked over to the door, ready to greet the next challenge. Or in this case, challenges.

Looking into a play corner of the room, he noticed Barney now sat alone by one of the bookshelves, abandoned by Alex who was deeply involved in smashing cars with Robert.

"I don't wanna go in!" Two identical blondes were pushed into the room by what had to be their father. One cried, the other giggled.

Jeff went through his greeting, this time emphasizing the fact that he was a special helper for Miss Allison. He placed a name tag on each girl as the father made a hasty retreat. With efficient speed, Jeff moved the crying one over to a seat near the green trash can. Rolling his shoulders, he figured she must like to throw things in it. Maybe it calmed her down.

Two seconds later, the blonde standing next to him heaved. Jeff cringed. She'd just puked on his wing-tipped shoe. An Italian one, very expensive, and not used to harsh treatment.

"Allison, help me, please!" Jeff yelled.

With her eyebrows raised, Allison quickly came over to where he stood. "Need my help already?"

Jeff pointed to his foot. "What's this all about?"

Allison swiveled her head from one twin to the other. "You have the girls mixed up. The one who just landed a deposit on your shoe is Tina. That's why I said to sit her next to the trashcan. She does this every morning."

"But she wasn't the one crying. She skipped into the room."

"Uh-huh," Allison grunted out as she knelt to comfort Tina. "We do this every day, don't we, honey?"

"I hate school," a soft whimpering voice answered.

"Stay put," Allison ordered Jeff. "You too, Tina. Rina, you go play. I'll grab some paper towels." She turned and sprinted into the kitchen.

With his head raised to the heavens, Jeff heaved a sigh and mumbled, "Where else would we possibly go?"

He could hear her explosion of laughter once Allison entered the kitchen. Obviously, she was amused as he quickly morphed from a rock-solid executive to a clueless caregiver. Crap. Why didn't he know more about kids? Maybe showing his vulnerable side would appeal to her. He could be helpless and outfoxed by preschoolers but still manage to keep his cool. Maybe the kids would warm up to him in time. Susan kept smiling and waving at him, so she sure seemed to like him.

Jeff noticed Allison peeking out of the doorway. Robert had lost his sneaker and needed help to get it back on. Jeff held the shoe in his hands, trying his hardest to undo a triple knot. He talked to the four-year-old as he worked, and the young boy listened intently while nodding his head a few times.

Allison finally exited the kitchen and jogged to where Jeff, Tina, and Robert stood.

"Here," she announced as she exchanged some paper towels for the tennis shoe. "I'm an old pro with Robert's famous knots. Why don't you clean your shoe? And Tina needs a little TLC at the moment, too."

"Sure thing. No problem." He winked at Robert as the child turned to walk away with Allison. "Don't forget what we talked about. Okay, buddy?"

The child tipped his head in agreement. Allison looked from Robert to Jeff. "And just what words of wisdom did you give Robert?" she asked.

Jeff quirked an eyebrow at her question and noted her look of curiosity. "Sorry, Miss Allison. This is man talk. No women are allowed to know our secrets."

Damn, Allison thought. Did being nice to kids make a guy sexier to women? She'd heard that men going to parks with kids always attracted women. Maybe Jeff fell into the see-how-good-I-am-with-kids category.

Allison closed her eyes, inhaling then breathing out a loud exhale. There was no denying it. He'd gotten her all hot and bothered in the elevator without kids. If he had this adoring attribute to add to his appealing and sexy charisma, how would she resist him when every fiber in her body itched to do that lap dance again?

Ignoring the urge to follow after Jeff and watch his every move or listen to his every conversation, she concentrated on setting out supplies. Damn, Jeff was fast becoming a major distraction that threatened to draw her attention to him each and every minute they were together. But their day had just started. Maybe his Randy Ryan nickname had been well-earned.

By nine fifteen, the other five children had arrived without incident. Jeff shouted orders for Welcome Circle Time right after Allison noticed him reading the chart.

She joined him in the circle and sat on the floor next to him. The wonderful scent of his aftershave drifted over to her and reminded Allison of sitting in that darkened, hot elevator. Touching his hip to hers didn't help her racing pulse or diminish thoughts of their passionate kiss.

"Mr. Jeff, would you take attendance?" She forced her voice to remain calm as she spoke and passed the attendance book to him. His warm hand covered hers as he grabbed it.

"Uh, sure. Just read the names?"

"Yes. The children know what to do." Lowering her voice, she said, "You can let go now."

After releasing her hand, he cleared his throat and called out the first name. "Alex Adams."

The child stood up. "Good morning. I'm Alex, and today I wanna play with trucks."

The rest of the children followed suit, each with a name and desire.

At her turn, Allison mentioned, "Good morning. I'm Miss Allison, and I want to bake cookies for snack today. I'll be able to do that because Mr. Jeff is here to be in charge and play with us."

The children clapped at the word cookies and then focused on their new leader.

After struggling to his feet, Jeff announced, "I'm Mr. Jeff, and I'm here to play with Miss Allison." He winked at her. "And I'd like to play with all of you, too."

Once again the children clapped. It was hard for Allison to hold back a slight smile curving up the corners of her mouth.

"So," he whispered to her as he turned, "what's next?"

Allison dazzled him with a bright smile. "Oh, you'll love this. Should be right up your alley."

"Now, Miss Allison. I don't see any elevator for me to get stuck in with a lovely companion again or all the hoopla that came along with it. Can't charm my charges here," he pointed to the children, "now can I?"

She raised her head a notch. Through gritted teeth, she answered, "We agreed to forget the elevator. This has nothing to do with sitting in your lap and—"

Allison swiveled her head from his direction to ten pairs of eyes, each trained on her and her every word. Every fiber in her body tensed as she made a desperate effort to find the correct words to say.

With a calm tone, she said, "I of course mean that there's no elevator in this room, so we can all sit by each other with our hands folded in our own laps."

"I thought you said something else but I guess I was wrong," Jeff stated. A devilish grin appeared on his face, and he rubbed his hands together. "Okay. Let's start this next adventure."

"Of course, Mr. Jeff. You go first. Time for Show and Tell. Since I don't think you brought anything to show, I'm sure the kids would just love to hear about your job. You know, like at your exciting board meetings. Tell us how hard you work, what you do, etc." She fluttered her eyelashes a few times for effect.

A look of panic flashed on his face. Allison knew wheels were churning in his corporate-oriented brain as he frantically searched for tidbits to share with his audience...the ones sucking thumbs, twisting hair, and wiggling on their rear ends.

A slow smile covered his face. "Sure. Okay, well, here goes. I didn't bring anything to show, so I'll tell you about my work. I have a big office and lots of people come to see me. I used to play football and loved running around like you guys probably like to do. Hey. Why don't we play tag later? I can be it and chase you guys and maybe catch Miss Allison. Won't that be fun?"

A chorus of kiddie giggles and laughter echoed through the room as he sat down.

"Thank you, Mr. Jeff. Maybe we'll have time for your wonderful suggestion later today," Allison remarked. Damn. No matter what she tried throwing his way, he was adapting to their daycare routine too nicely. Would she lose their bet? Would he disappear out of her life without a second thought?

Allison removed her gaze from Jeff to survey the kids. One hand went up.

"Mr. Gef," Susan asked as she tried to hide her face with her hands. "Do you have a girlfriend?"

"Not right now, Susan." He glanced at Allison and grinned before turning back to face the kids. "But I'm looking for one."

The rest of the kids took their turns at Show and Tell and when it was over they left for free play. Allison tugged Jeff over to one side of the room. "What are you trying to do? Ruin my business?"

Furrowing his brow, Jeff responded, "Huh? What are you talking about? Are you nipping sherry back there in that kitchen?"

With a huff, she answered, "If the kids can figure out that there's something going on, so can everyone else, including their parents."

"So what?" Jeff bent down to shove an errant truck out of his way.

"I could lose clients if they think I'm paying more attention to you than the children."

"Allison," Jeff said in a seductive tone, "You and I know we connected on Friday. Remember? You, me, the heat, kissing, lap dancing." He stretched out an arm, and his fingers ran feathery strokes up and down her arm. "Isn't there something going on between us?"

Her body cried out "absolutely," but her heart held back, remembering the past and her ex-boyfriend's betrayal. Michael was the reason she'd quit her last job and taken Aunt Abigail's place at Ryan's Rugrats. Hell, she'd lost her dignity and self-respect to one smooth operator in a very short period of time.

Was Jeff like Michael?

Tossing a wayward curl away from her face with the back of her hand, Allison searched Jeff's face, hoping to find something more genuine and trustworthy than what she'd experienced from her last love. Love? She shook her head to clear her thoughts. It was way too soon to even use that word in a sentence with Jeff's name.

"Jeff, I don't know how to answer you. We barely know each other."

"Our kiss meant something. Sitting on me had to catch your attention as much as my reaction."

Shards of heat scattered throughout her body as she recalled their tight embrace and tongue-dancing kiss. His heartbeat had sped with hers, and both had panted in passionate need.

"I can't think about that now." She glanced around the room. "Anyway, we'll be plenty busy just corralling the ten of them all day. Remember? We're surrounded by kids."

His eyes blazed. "I'd rather corral you and be busy doing something more grown-up."

"Please," she begged and placed her hand over his. "We have a job to do, and you have to prove you can handle it."

Some of the fire disappeared from his gaze, but he twisted his hand and gave a squeeze. "I plan to win. Everything."

"And so do I." She spoke her sentence to his retreating back as he walked to the coloring area where two children waited for supplies. Allison raised her heated hand to her cheek and savored the warm sensation his contact had set off. Touching him was a mistake. But, damn if she didn't enjoy it.

At five-twenty, Jeff lay spread-eagle in the middle of the room, flat on the carpet and surrounded by an array of toy trucks.

"I'm never moving from this spot. Throw me some of those fabulous cookies you made, cover me with one of the blankets, turn off the lights, and go away. I'll see you tomorrow."

Allison tiptoed over to Jeff's side. After placing her hands on her hips, she shook her head in fake dismay. "My, my. Did we have a rough day?"

"Just assure me it's really over and they've all left. Don't toy with my sanity."

He looked pitiful. Splatters of chalk dust from a venture outside in creative sidewalk art covered his rumpled blue Armani pants. Red crayon marks, courtesy of Tanner, stained his once-starched shirt.

Jeff's silk tie, a red, blue, and silver concoction, remained where Debbie had left it after she "borrowed" it from his suit jacket. She'd tied dolls to it to play mountain climbing with Rachel.

Allison loved the new look. The one of a man who'd barely survived a new experience and lived to tell it. He'd jumped right in, hit the ground with the kids, and still managed to maintain a sense of humor.

Not to mention, he looked devilishly handsome, making it hard for her to squelch the urge to get on the floor with him. Comforting Jeff, experiencing the warmth of his embrace and the passion of his demanding kisses danced as an urgent desire in her head. Damn him.

She really thought he'd bolt when he accidentally tripped over Austen. The tyke had kicked him hard in the shins, then cried and wiped his nose on Jeff's pants as the hobbling man had tried to comfort him.

Jeff closed his eyes. His breathing slowed as Allison watched the rise and fall of his muscular chest. Lord, she longed to have her head near his heart, so she could listen to it beat a rhythm lovers would fall into sync with. Her heartbeat would mimic his, speeding up as they both gave in to their desires.

"It's safe now. All the kids are happily on their way home. You did okay for a first-timer."

Jeff opened one eye and glared at her. "Okay? Just okay? I think a Purple Heart is in order here."

"You mean for the kids for putting up with you? Or, maybe you mean for me for surviving your charming company and all the help you gave." She laughed and sank to her knees.

"Ha ha. You know what I meant." He got up on one elbow and turned his body toward her. "I surprised you, didn't I?"

"Hmm. I guess so. Although, taking your accomplishment seriously would work better if you didn't have pink finger paint in your hair."

She stretched out her hand to his head and leaned over toward him. Her pulse quickened as she ran her fingertips through his hair. Allison recognized the yearning that surfaced in his dark brown eyes and realized the same one railroaded throughout her own body. When his arm swung out to pull her to him, she didn't hesitate.

Chapter Five

One kiss. That's all *I'll give him. Just one kiss.*
Jeff tightened his embrace around her as Allison easily slipped along the length of his body. His kiss spoke of urgency and lust.

Maybe two kisses.

She could no more pull away from him than she could will her heart to stop beating. She wanted this. She wanted him. She wanted Jeff to—

"Am I interrupting?"

At Elizabeth Ryan's unexpected question, Allison rolled over to the side and hastily rose to her feet. Jeff plopped back down on the carpet.

"Mother, what the hell are you doing here? Checking up on me?"

With a "humph," Mrs. Ryan glared at her son and strode inside the room. "What a ridiculous thing to say. Keeping tabs on you would be a monumental job. I'd need a complete staff to do that. I came to see Allison."

At the mention of her name, Allison cringed and pasted a nervous smile on her face. "We were just, uh—"

"Practicing CPR. Allison resuscitated me after the long, hard day I had. Right?" Jeff smirked in her direction.

After exhaling a loud sigh, she pivoted to face Elizabeth. "No, we were kissing. I think I probably went crazy cooped up in here all day with your son and just decided I'd either have to kill him or kiss him."

"Don't worry, dear." Elizabeth walked over to her and patted her hand. "I understand completely."

"Hey! Ladies, I can hear every word." A rakish grin formed on his face. "So," he aimed a narrow-eyed look at Allison, "it's kill or kiss, hmm? I'm thinking I did extremely well today."

Elizabeth said, "Jeffrey, that statement would appear more credible if you weren't spread out on the floor looking like a gladiator who'd just fought off twenty lions and somehow managed to survive. I'm assuming you did because you're still breathing."

"Thanks for your support, Mom."

A fantasy image of Jeff as a gladiator wearing skimpy outfits that highlighted his bulging muscles flashed through Allison's head and sent a rush of heat coursing through her body. She needed solitude to escape the magnetic pull of his kisses and her own craving to satisfy a more lust-filled exploration of his body.

"You said you came to see me?" Allison asked in a hurried tone.

"You forgot this in Jeff's office last week." The older woman rummaged through her purse and handed Allison a lipstick.

"Oh. Thank you. Sorry you had to make the trip here."

"No trouble for me at all. I was on my way home from the mall and—"

"You don't live in this direction," Jeff interrupted. "You're here to spy."

"I am not." Elizabeth sniffed and aimed a stare of disapproval in her son's direction. "What I was going to say is I thought I'd come here before I make a quick stop at the Archbishop's. Then I'll be going home."

"I'm sorry to sound ungrateful, but it's getting late. I really do need to go." Allison prayed they'd get the hint and leave.

"Go," Jeff offered in a tired voice from his resting spot on the floor. "I'll finish putting things away and lock up. See you in the morning."

Allison almost gave in to the urge to stay and help. But being around him left her vulnerable to temptation. She'd have to cool her hunger and desire for him, so reining in her passion had to be accomplished. As much as her body yearned for his caresses and fueled her desire to touch him, she had to win their challenge.

"Jeff, dear, are you going to move soon?" Elizabeth said after Allison disappeared out the door.

He sat up, running a hand through paint-splattered hair. "Yes. Why don't you take off? I'll finish here like I told her and go home. Assuming I can walk, drive, and stay awake."

"What happened to your tie and shoes? I don't see them."

"Simple explanations. Tina decided to throw-up on my shoe and after trying to clean it, I thought it would be better to go shoeless." He guffawed. "My tie," he pointed to the left, "is over there, transformed into a rope for a game of Dolls Climbing Mount Bookcase. Any more questions?"

"Why are you on the floor?"

"The boys and I decided to play kill the giant. You'll be happy to know I was chosen to be the bad guy by a unanimous vote."

With a look of true concern, Elizabeth stated, "You look drained. I'm worried about you. Was it really very bad?"

"I never imagined how hard this could be. You want the honest truth?"

Elizabeth nodded. "Of course."

Jeff bent sideways as he nabbed a nearby truck. "I don't know if I can last the week." He shrugged. "I'm already beginning to see how this place is too small and why Allison wants to make improvements and expand. And, she mentioned the ridiculous rent she has to come up with for next month."

With muscles aching all over his body, Jeff got to his feet. "Maybe I should just admit defeat, consider Allison's financial plan, and be out of her hair." He glanced back at his mother. "I don't think I'm rugrat material."

"Maggie already told me about the center's financial difficulties.

You can always give financial aid, but I've never known you to back out of a challenge so quickly."

Jeff stared at his mother as her words sunk into his head. "Actually, I've never backed out of a challenge, period. Even if it meant losing."

Elizabeth looked at her watch. "It's getting late, so I'll be going. What have you decided to do?"

With a grin, he answered, "Good night, Mother. I'll figure this out."

After she left, Jeff rushed through the center and cleaned according to the list Allison had posted on the wall for him. He ached from too much unaccustomed activity forced on his body in one short day.

Yeah, he understood what Allison meant by not just babysitting. He'd actually looked over her e-mails a few times so he knew of her financial plans and goals. Why the hell hadn't he just said yes?

He snorted. Maybe Maggie was right. The "old men" on the board had influenced his decision. And the daily reminder of seeing the Ryan's Rugrats sign as he entered his building struck a guilty chord inside him. It was named after his company, and his employees benefited by using it.

After locking the building, he stretched before walking over to his car. He wouldn't give up because that might mean not being near Allison for the entire week. If he called it quits now, would she view him as weak, even if he did offer a partnership?

Keeping in her good graces and close to the woman whose kisses urged him to want more seemed like the right choice to make. He'd finish his week with the rugrats, keep her constantly by his side, and have a weekend to explore whatever relationship they might have together.

As Jeff arrived on Tuesday morning, Allison noticed he wore slacks and a T-shirt. "You look more dressed for the occasion. Ready for another round?"

"Certainly. I collapsed into bed as soon as I got home and slept through the night." He rubbed his hands together. "So, I'm ready for rugrats. Unless you're offering something else?"

"Not on your life. You're the enemy. Rugrats it is." She angled her head toward the wall. "Chart's up. Today's a special event day. Ready for a surprise?"

The smiling expression on his face drooped. "Give me the bad news straight up. I hate surprises, unless they involve beautiful women, me, and a deserted island."

With a sparkle in her eye and spring in her voice, Allison remarked, "It's field trip day."

After waiting for the kids to arrive, Jeff, Allison, Mary Jackson, and ten preschoolers headed for the daycare van. Once there, he carefully lifted each child in before jumping in himself. A date at the local post office loomed ahead.

Mrs. Jackson took the seat up front with Allison who was acting as the van's driver, leaving Jeff to sit between four rows of kids.

"Is everyone buckled in?" Allison asked.

A kiddie chorus of "yes" floated through the air. Jeff pulled himself out from the back row of seats where he'd helped the last four kids into their seat belts.

"Mr. Gef, will you hold my hand?" Susan asked.

"Sure." He sat next to her and took her small hand in his.

Giggles erupted from the row behind him.

"Uh-oh, Mr. Jeff's in love," yelled Robert.

Jeff turned to face his accuser. "We're just friends, Robert. Look out the window and enjoy the ride."

Allison kept sneaking peeks in the rearview mirror at the handsome hunk mixed in with his tiny partners. She glanced at Mary and made an effort to curtail any outburst of laughter.

"We'll be there in a few minutes. Mr. Jeff, did you have a song you'd like us all to sing?"

He glared into the rearview mirror. "The only one I can think of at the spur of the moment has something to do with ninety-nine bottles of something on a wall."

Mary unsuccessfully tried to stifle a giggle.

"Hmm. I don't think the kids know that one", Allison remarked. "How about Old MacDonald? Just come up with all sorts of animal sounds."

Jeff eased into a rendition of the song, and the kids gave their enthusiastic support. Slightly off-key, his deep, husky voice paved the way for his version. The children followed his lead, adding sounds and different words to mimic their leader.

After being serenaded by ten angelic voices and one all-male baritone, Allison coasted the van into the post office parking lot. Before allowing the children to exit, she turned to Jeff and said, "Why don't you remind us of our good visiting manners and rules."

Jeff's face paled. Allison could hear the gears and wheels grinding in his handsome head as he searched for the answers. Not feeling the least bit sorry for him, she remained silent, figuring he should have read the chart.

"Oh, yeah. The rules." He grinned at her and Mary and then turned toward the kids. Jeff pulled a crumpled paper from his pocket and began reading. "Listen up, you guys. No running. Stay with your grownup. No yelling. Be polite." He glanced at Allison. "Did I forget anything?"

"No. I guess we're ready to go inside." While impressed that he'd remembered the rules, a slight wave of anxiety made her wonder if maybe he had a chance to win their challenge.

Jeff helped unbuckle and guide the children out of the van. Once on the sidewalk, Allison assigned each child to an adult's supervision and reminded them to hold hands while walking.

"Mr. Gef? Hold my hand." Susan reached for his hand.

"Sure thing, sweetie. Say, should I hold Miss Allison's hand, so she doesn't get lost?" He winked at the giggling little girl.

After watching Jeff's handling of Susan, Allison gave the child a smile and then glared at him. "I'll be holding hands with Marcus and Alex today. You can hang onto Robert and watch Rina and

Tina as they walk next to you."

"So I get to escort four kids while you two only get three apiece?"

"Absolutely, Mr. Jeff. After all, you're in charge."

Jeff thanked the field trip gods that their post office venture was almost over and accomplished without a hitch. His plan to go to the post office, tour with the kids, and go back to the center had materialized into an uneventful schedule for him to follow.

As he held hands with Susan and Robert while Rina and Tina skipped in front of him, an errant squirrel appeared to create chaos in the short walking distance to the van. Before he had a chance to react, the twins began screaming and ran into him. Susan and Robert joined in the excitement, and all four children pushed his body as they tried to cling to him.

Jeff managed to loosen their grips on him before tripping backwards. With a loud, "Oomph," he landed next to a rose bush and tore a hole in his pants, almost completely ripping off his right back pocket.

"Are you okay?" Allison asked as Mary gathered the children near her.

Jeff stood and dusted himself off, trying to hide his embarrassment. Falling flat on his butt wasn't part of his carefully laid-out plans.

Not only was he nursing a bruised rear end, but his underwear showed. The ones with the red and purple smiley faces his sister had given him last Christmas. *And may God bless you, Sister Margaret Mary.*

"I'm fine. Just sore. Let's get back to the center." He hurried to the van and began lifting the kids get in. "Must be time for lunch pretty soon." Out of the corner of his eye, he saw Allison staring at him.

"We could always take you to the emergency room," she suggested. "You don't have to be macho about this."

He lifted the last child into the van before turning to Allison and whispering his reply in her ear. "I'm not gonna lounge around in some hospital so you can say I lost. I'll be fine. Wanna kiss my boo-boo?"

Allison's cheeks flushed a lovely shade of red. She tugged him away from the van. "If you think I'd ever kiss your rear end, I have a bridge to sell you in New York."

Jeff waved his hand at her, the one he'd slammed on the concrete sidewalk as he'd tried to break his fall. Scratches covered his palm. "This," he put his injured hand closer to her face, "is what I wanted kissed."

Her eyes opened wide. "Oh, just get in the van and let's go. We still have to feed the kids and get the afternoon group back here by two."

"What? We have to do this all again?" he asked as she walked to the driver's side of the van.

They returned to the center and fed their charges. After lunch, Jeff helped Allison clean up. The half-day switch had already taken place, so five children had left and five more took their places.

"Same routine this afternoon? Preferably minus the squirrel bit?" Jeff asked.

"We'll only be taking five to the post office. What can I say? Stop attracting squirrels. And, since I don't want to leave you here alone with the ones who went this morning, Mary will rest with them."

Rest. The word conjured up a vision of laying on mats, eyes closing, and time to actually relax. And if the kids slept along with him, so what?

"I'd be happy to stay put. Five kids won't be a problem. You ladies go on ahead and enjoy the second tour."

Allison shook her finger under his nose. "Oh, no, you don't. You're in charge, and it's your responsibility to be with the kids if they're out. You're lucky I don't send you alone with them." She batted her eyelashes and grinned. "Lord knows how many you'd lose."

"Mr. Gef? I like your smiley faces." Susan handed him a picture and scurried away as she giggled.

"What's that?" Allison leaned in closer to him.

"Obviously she knows her colors. See? She made what I assume are red and purple smiley faces." Jeff patted the area of his torn pocket.

Allison laughed. "You're motivating her creative instincts. Great job. Maybe I'll have it framed for you. Then we can frame your boxers and hang them right next to Susan's masterpiece. Interesting conversational pieces."

"Uh-huh. Laugh all you want. You're just jealous because she likes me and isn't afraid to show it."

Allison's whole body shook with laughter again. Jeff longed to hold her tight and start more adult one-on-one games, out of public view and more private for fantasy lovemaking encounters.

"I have a sewing kit in the kitchen, so maybe I can fix your pocket before we leave again. If you take off your pants—"

"You want my pants?"

"Shhh! Keep your voice down," she hissed. "Look, you can run around with your faces smiling on the whole world for all I care." She sniffed and raised her gorgeous head a few inches. "Just don't be surprised if people start gawking at you."

Jeff's attempt at teasing Allison hadn't worked, and he guessed he'd tested her patience enough for the time being. However, he couldn't ignore how her fiery temper emphasized her beautiful eyes and escalated his desire to have her in his arms and on his lap again.

"Sorry. You're trying to be helpful, and I'm not making this easy. Fine. I'll hop into the bathroom and take them off. Just be quick about it. Okay?"

"Sure. The sooner you're decent, the faster we can leave."

Jeff ducked into the boy's room and surveyed the extra low facilities made to cater to tiny male bodies. He removed his pants and checked the reflection of his flashy underwear in the mirror. With a sigh, he shuffled over to the door and peeked out.

Mary had the ten children settled for a story, and Allison

leaned by his opened door, holding out her hand.

"Here. And don't let any of the kids come in while you sew."

Grabbing his pants, she replied, "I'll go as fast as I can. Stay put."

After closing the door, Jeff slouched against the bathroom wall. "Like I have a choice?" he mumbled to himself. He rubbed his face with his hands. What the hell would the rest of his day be like?

Chapter Six

After the last child left for the evening, Jeff sat on a tiny chair with his head hung back, legs outstretched, and arms dangling at his sides. Allison saw his eyes close and wondered if he'd fall asleep.

"Hi, Allison." A cheerful Maggie entered the center.

"Oh, hi." Allison put a finger to her lips and pointed at Jeff. "I think he's sleeping."

Maggie looked from Allison to Jeff and back to Allison again. "You don't look tired. What's wrong with him?"

One eye on the reclining man popped open. "Did my mother send you here to check on me?"

Rolling her eyes, Maggie answered, "Of course not. I have three papers for you to sign, and I figured I'd save you a trip to the office."

Unbending and stretching his body into an upright position, Jeff trudged over to his secretary. "Sorry. What am I signing? I don't think I can focus."

Allison thought he resembled Robert when the child pouted just before throwing a tantrum. When that happened, she assigned the little boy to a time out in a corner.

Even in this condition, Jeff appealed to her. The distracting image of him in his smiling boxers had jumped into her head all afternoon. She'd even stuck her finger three times with the needle while sewing his pocket back in place.

Maggie interrupted Allison's wandering thoughts. "These are the contracts you negotiated last week. I just need your signature to send them through."

"Right." Jeff grabbed the papers and hunched over one of the small tables so he could sign them. "Here."

"Are you okay?" Maggie took the papers.

"We've been extra busy today," Allison admitted.

Jeff gave a sad grin. "Just tired but I'll recharge after a few weeks sleep. No problem."

"Yes, well, thanks for signing these. I'll be going. Bye, Allison, Jeff."

"We all should leave. Ready, Jeff?"

"Yeah."

"See you tomorrow." Allison waited for him to head out before turning off the lights.

He gave her a backhanded wave and slowly walked away. Abruptly pivoting in her direction, Jeff marched over to where she stood. Before Allison could utter a sound, he hugged her in a tight embrace.

His lips met hers, and his tongue traced her bottom lip, urging her to open to him. Allison lost all sense of time as Jeff deepened their kiss. Accepting her heart's desire and hunger for his caresses, she wrapped her arms around his neck and pulled him closer.

Too soon to satisfy her yearning, he gently pushed her away. "Women," he mumbled. He ran his hand through his hair and shook his head. "I'd better go."

Allison watched him leave while rubbing her swollen lips, still tingling from his touch. Her heart pounded, and she burned with a lusty desire for more intimate contact. For a split second, she wondered if losing the bet would be worth having him all to herself for a weekend.

"Men," she whispered to the empty hall as she left the building.

She got into her car and tried to concentrate on driving, but thoughts of Jeff kept popping into her head. At her apartment parking lot, she got out of her car, walked briskly to her door, and opened it. Longing for a cool drink, Allison poured herself an iced tea and dropped into an overstuffed chair.

Maybe, just maybe, she was driving the man so far away he'd never consider giving her a second look. That kiss still meant he wanted her, didn't it? It didn't seem like a goodbye caress. *Keep focused*, she chided herself. She couldn't afford to think about her relationship with Jeff as anything other than a business proposition.

Business. Right. Damn if he hadn't unnerved her at every turn. He was kind, sexy, and boiled her blood. He offered all the things a woman would say about a man she desired. Allison hoped to permanently relegate Michael and his betrayal to the past and take a chance at trusting another man again by easing Jeff into her life. But not because he'd won a bet. She wanted his caresses because he wanted her—just because she was Allison Minetti.

Chugging down a cool swig of her drink, she melted at endearing images of him holding little Susan's hand and making the child feel special. Actually, all the kids loved him. And in his own way, he probably loved them, too. He'd quickly morphed into family material before her eyes—the type she'd always wanted and needed.

How did he feel about marriage and the whole family bit? Should she trust her instincts and follow her heart while ignoring the logical, saner part that longed to keep possible heartache at bay?

A bleary-eyed Jeff rolled out of bed and checked his alarm clock to make sure it hadn't gone off early. His body, sapped of energy, buzzed with warning bells. It couldn't be six already. He needed more sleep and additional time to rest his weary bones.

Squinting as he tried to focus on the clock face, he prayed it would read any number of hours earlier than when he planned to arise. *Nope. Six it is. Shit.* He flopped back on the bed and considered the possibility of saying, "The hell with it." He could give up and sleep through the day. His mind, taken over by devious demons, reasoned out the pros to his stay-home scenario. He hadn't had a vacation, a real one, in three years. He worked overtime on an almost daily basis. Wasn't he entitled to play hooky after running his business so successfully for the past five years?

His other side, the angelic one, offered the cons. Being a dedicated professional had railroaded him up the ladder of success. He'd always given two-hundred percent, which paid off in his company's ratings and longevity. Super executives didn't just give up. They played hardball, lost sleep, and sacrificed their time, and yes, their lives, for their businesses.

But the biggest con would be losing to Allison. Or, just plain losing her. Would she think him weak or be satisfied getting what she wanted and forget all about him in the process? Hell, she didn't kiss like she'd forget him, but he'd been fooled before. He'd experienced Laura.

Jeff forced himself into an upright position and shook off memories of his ex. He begged his body to find the strength to try one more day. He could do it. He wanted to do it.

He wanted Allison, so he had to do it.

"Good morning." Jeff offered his greeting as he entered the center, armed with a steaming cup of strong black coffee.

"Mmm. Smells good. I do have coffee here, you know." Allison gave him one of her adorable smiles as she tacked up the chart for the day.

"Yeah, I know. All decaf, washed-out stuff. But this is real coffee. Super high-test mud. It'll either kill me or keep me wired throughout the day."

"Hmm. Can't say I'd care much for dead bodies cluttering up the floor." Allison shrugged. "The kids would probably take it in stride, though, grab blocks and build castles on Mr. Jeff Mountain. Or they could turn you into a train station, running engines all over your body." She fluttered her eyelashes at him.

"I've already been a dead giant, so I'll forgo the mountain and trains. I'll handle being wired." He turned toward the daily chart.

As Allison headed for the walk-in supply closet, she tossed out, "Be sure to read item three."

"The first two," he read them quickly to himself, "yeah, I already know. Thanks. No surprises there." He tilted his body closer to the paper, mouthing words in disbelief.

"Huh? Did you say something?" Allison's question came from within the closet.

Jeff swiveled his head in the direction of squeaking sounds coming just in time to witness Allison wheeling out a folded-up crib. His voice raised an octave as he asked, "Diaper Day?"

"Yep. We offer care to all ages under six. Every Wednesday and Friday we get some little ones."

His first instinct was to sprint for the door. He hadn't expected infants. Shit. He had enough trouble managing preschoolers, but how would he handle babies? A sense of panic quickened his heart rate, and he longed for a soothing, comforting hug. But he couldn't trust himself to let her go if Allison offered one.

Jeff hurried over to where she stood. "How many miniature rugrats?"

"Today—here, grab this end—we'll have five infants and Joel, Austen, Tanner, Rachel, and Debbie all day. No switches done at noon."

"All day? Anyone coming to help us?"

"Janet comes today," Allison grinned at him. "It's just you and me until she gets here, oh fearless leader. C'mon. Help me get out the other cribs."

Jeff followed her in a sleepwalking haze. He'd need more coffee to make it through the day. Hell, could he make it through the first hour?

Allison's voice grabbed his attention. "Get that crib on your left. You saw me set up the first one, so it shouldn't be too hard for you to figure out by yourself."

They both wheeled out cribs and placed them on the far side of the room leaving space for the older children to play.

Jeff asked, "Won't it be too noisy? How can babies sleep in here?"

"Kids are adaptable. They can handle it. Plus, the five running around today are usually the quieter ones."

Jeff furrowed his brow. "Are we talking about the same rugrats I've already met? Quiet? I swear they must drink the same stuff I've had all morning."

Allison took a deep breath. "Look, it won't be hard. Follow the schedule. Let's get the last two cribs up before the kids come, or you'll be holding them all day."

Jeff dashed with her to the closet and worked faster. They finished placing the five cribs into their positions in the rest area seconds before three bundles of joy arrived. The infants were placed on a blanket on the floor. With jangled nerves, Jeff loomed over them and stared.

"Will they move? Do I need to tape them down or something?"

Laughing, Allison said, "Those three will pretty much stay put. And I think the state frowns on taping kids."

"So I just stand here?"

"No. You just sit over there on the "big people" rocking chair and watch them while you feed Dawn."

"Huh?" Jeff dropped into the seat and gazed at his three miniature charges squirming and gurgling on the floor. Since they were quiet and content for the moment, he willed his breathing to slow to a normal pace.

"Stay there, Mr. Jeff. Dawn's mother is coming through the door. She'll bring the baby over to you." Allison smirked. "You're sitting in our designated feeding chair."

Feeding chair? Why couldn't Allison sit there instead? Preferably on his lap while she did?

"Jeff, this is Roberta. She'll explain what to do. I need to answer the phone." Allison rushed off heading for the kitchen as

Anything You Can Do

a pink-clad bundle landed in his arms.

"I think it's just wonderful that you offered to help out here this week. Not many men would do that."

"Yeah," he gulped and offered an insincere smile. "Allison can be very persuasive."

Jeff held the baby as Roberta unwrapped the child from her blanket. She handed Jeff a bottle.

"She's all set. Changed her before we left home. I expressed plenty of fresh milk for later. I'll just go put the container in the refrigerator."

Juggling the bottle he'd been handed, Jeff almost dropped it as the words expressed and milk registered in his brain. His new task included holding an infant dressed in a frilly pink and green lace dress and feeding her a bottle full of breast milk.

It wouldn't be so bad if it was his and Allison's child. The fleeting thought took him by surprise. It was a definite contrast to his ex. He'd never conjured up a vision of Laura as the motherly type. A cry from the bundle of joy wiggling in his arms broke through his daydream. Jeff glanced at the bodies on the carpet and considered himself lucky they still remained calm.

"Okay kid, here goes. Keep in mind I haven't done this before," he whispered as he inserted the bottle's nipple into the child's mouth. It was easier than he expected. Dawn did her part, and once again, quiet reined in Jeff's corner of the world.

When he turned his head, he saw Roberta and Allison deep in some type of discussion. The baby's mother waved then exited the room. Allison strolled over to him.

"Boy, this is sure strange. The other five kids will be out today. Two parents forgot to tell me they're taking vacation time, and Joel's sick."

"Isn't he the one who kept sneezing on me?"

Allison frowned. "Yeah, you're right. But the other two, well, the parents said something about a special project out of town and taking the kids with them. Know anything about it?"

Keeping his concentration trained on feeding Dawn, Jeff shrugged and offered, "People always travel for business. There are any number of projects happening at one time. I travel three or four times a month myself."

"Oh." She tilted her head, studying him. "You look very natural doing that. I think you've been holding out on me. In your past life, you were probably a nanny or a governess."

"Cute. I guess it's not so hard. What about the carpet crawlers? Do I have to feed them, too? Or are you gonna do anything else except answer phones and watch me do all the work?"

Dawn stopped sucking on her bottle and let out a wail.

"What? Isn't she supposed to finish this?" Jeff held up the baby's bottle.

"You need to burp her." Allison sat on the floor and "coochie-cooed" the three babies lying there.

Holding the baby away from him, Jeff stared into the tear-stained face of another female he'd never really understand. Even this one had demands: feed her, hold her, burp her. He shuddered. What if "change her" was next on the list?

"So kid, go on and burp."

"It might work better if you hold her up on your chest near your shoulder. Be sure to support her head while you pat her gently on the back a few times. She should burp then," Allison suggested.

"Sure, easy for you to say."

Jeff did as instructed. After six pats, the child belched. With the sound, other stuff spilled out, too. On his shirt. On his shoulder. Down his front.

Surprised at the deposit seeping through to his skin, Jeff said, "First Tina with my shoe. Now this one who can't possibly hate me yet decides she doesn't like my shirt. What is it? Doesn't she like the color?"

While laughing, Allison picked up John, stood up, and rocked him in her arms. "Why didn't you put the burp cloth on your shoulder? And all the girls don't hate you. Susan adores you. And your smiley underwear."

"Yeah, laugh all you want. Where's this cloth you're talking about?"

She grabbed it from under his arm and handed it to him.

"Thanks. Too little too late."

"Put her on her back in the pink crib. You can go and wipe that off. I'll be fine here with everyone."

Jeff placed the child in her crib, amazed at the happy look on the baby's face.

"I notice you didn't mention how you feel about me."

Allison gave him a sideways glance, one that struck him as both fetching and seductive. A burning desire for her flared in the pit of his stomach and traveled lower down his body, regardless of the fact that infants surrounded them. If he tried to kiss her senseless, the mini-rugrats wouldn't be able to tell.

She winked, and her voice came out as barely above a whisper. "I love your smiley shorts too."

"Oh, I see. It's my underwear you're after."

"I've brought Angela."

Jeff and Allison turned to the left where Angela's mother stood, obviously privy to their previous conversation. Allison hurried to talk to her.

When the mother left, Jeff glared at Allison. "Why did you tell her about my underwear fiasco?"

"It seemed honesty would be better than trying to make up some explanation for your stupid comment." She raised her chin and held her head up high.

He waved a finger in her direction. "There's something going on in that sabotaging brain of yours. I'm here for the duration, no matter what you throw at me. Go on. Give me your best shot. I can handle anything."

"Oh? I'm glad to hear that. I called Janet and told her to stay home. Since only five kids are here today, you and I should be able to handle things."

"That's it? Five kids all day, and you call that a challenge?"

"No," she grunted as she placed John back on the blanket, lifted Brian, and handed him to Jeff. "He's your next challenge," she said, nodding her head at the child in his arms. "Change him."

The morning flew by with both of them rocking, feeding, changing, or just watching the five infants. Jeff had to admit it wasn't half as bad as he expected. Well, he could do without the changing part, but after being squirted by Brian, he'd learned how to be more careful when changing the boys. Still, the babies had kept them busy. He shuddered to think how adding five mobile tykes to the mixture would have created chaos. Even if another adult had shown up to help.

Jeff had to admit he was fascinated at the infant exercises they did with the babies but also relieved when it was time to put them in their cribs. Allison dimmed the lights and turned on a light show machine that reflected on the ceiling over the cribs. After putting a CD in her player, soft music filtered throughout the main room. Then she invited him into the kitchen.

"They won't all sleep right now, but they're usually pretty content with the lights and music for awhile. Hungry? I brought some ravioli to heat up for us. Hope you like it."

Her eager look and caring concern softened his already mushy heart. "I'll eat anything. Iron stomachs come in handy. How good a cook are you?"

"How good do I need to be?"

Muscles tightened in his body as heat switches everywhere turned to the on position. A myriad of meanings for the word good describing Allison streamed through his head. Good kisser. Good in the dark. Good in bed.

"How good can you be?" he asked in a husky tone. He longed to find out if her thoughts headed in the same direction as his.

"I'm always good," she drawled.

His heart pounded, and Jeff pulled in shallow breaths. "Then show me."

Allison darted her eyes from the microwave where she'd just

popped in their meal to the opened door where the cribs were visible. She wiped her hands on a towel and gave him a saucy look. Jeff hugged her to him in one swift rush. He lowered his lips to hers. Sparks flew between them and charged the air surrounding them. Her breathing quickened as it raced to match his and heightened the fervor and fury of their passion. His heart beat wildly, and he could feel hers racing to meet his tempo.

As they kissed, Allison's brain ran amok with questions. Would this lead to something right now? Did they have time for this? Did she want there to be time? She thought and discarded scores of reasons to head in either direction. Yes, yes, yes. She wanted him and now could work. No, no, no. This was wrong. All the rational reasons she'd already thought of paraded through her mind.

Her body lacked any hint of the control she attempted to possess. Her senses took off running at his caresses, and every one of his strokes burned her where he touched. She panted with a desire she'd long ago banished to the furthest recesses of her mind and existence. Michael had done a number on her, and that wouldn't be repeated.

Tiny warning bells jingled in her head and signaled trouble ahead if they continued at the lightning speed their mutual passion dictated. Someone had to be in control and say, "Stop." Allison's heart sank behind barrier walls in an attempt to ward off the attacking passion. Her body cried out, "Full speed ahead," while her head gave in to more practical and logical restraints.

Ending their kisses, she pulled away and rested her head on his shoulder. Still held tightly in his embrace, she moved her arms from around his neck to circle his waist. She willed her breathing to return to normal. This was too soon. Jeff's ardor curled her toes and drugged her into wanting more of him.

"I guess that's a no." His voice came out in shuddered gasps.

"The kids are in the next room. Anyone can walk in here at any moment. Did you think we could continue?"

"Nah. Too risky. We need to find a more solitary spot and

carry on from where we left off."

"And what about the kids? We can't just leave them here."

Sighing deeply, he kissed her forehead and then stepped back. "You're right. I don't know what came over me." He winked. "It must be the lack of food."

"I guess I better feed you then." Allison turned to grab the ravioli out of the microwave.

"Sounds good, but I'd still rather nibble on you."

They ate quickly and spoke about their next few hours at the center. With an edge of relief, Allison welcomed the quiet setting and nonverbal agreement to ease their mutual attraction from further discussion. Angela's wail set them in motion, and they jogged to the crib area.

"She sure has a lusty cry for a girl, doesn't she?" Jeff swung his head in the direction of the crying child.

"They all do. We'll check for diaper changes and see who's hungry. Just leave the ones that are asleep alone for now."

Within the hour, all fives babies were awake and ready for attention.

Jeff mentioned, "You know, this isn't half-bad. I can handle this."

Allison smiled, but her thoughts flew in another direction. He was doing well. Too well. He'd made it through three days of her dare. Full of guilt over wishing he'd fail and miffed he'd survived despite setbacks, she started visualizing an upcoming Friday consequence. Of course there were two more days, and they should be as hectic as the first two. He still had time to admit defeat, leave the center, and offer to give credence to her request for financial aid.

Something still troubled her about the missing five preschoolers and their sudden disappearance from the schedule. She'd never had more than one child absent at a time. Strange how that happened right when she kept tossing everything she could at him. Her gaze wandered over to the hunky male rocking a sleepy Dawn. He murmured something to the child and added a silly grin to his face.

Jeff epitomized the kind of man Allison wanted when she had children. Someone who would not only hold a baby but get involved in every aspect of caring for him or her. Someone not afraid to utter sweet nothings to a six-month-old. Someone willing to get on the floor and tickle tiny tummies and rub miniature fingers and toes.

But what about in other regards?

He was stubborn. He'd put off her many funding requests. Taking on her challenge had been gutsy. But did he do it to prove he had all the answers? He was vulnerable. She'd seen that side of him many times as each new crisis with the kids came up and he'd had to deal with it. Yesterday he'd seemed so tired Allison questioned his sanity at not admitting defeat.

And, he was damn sexy. No doubt about his attraction and her wanton reactions. But were his flirting and sexual innuendoes just for show, a ploy on his part to get her to forget her goal?

After giving herself a mental shake, Allison suddenly realized that the only sounds she heard were gurgling noises coming from the three babies in the playpen and the one on her lap. No constant squeak came from the rocker Jeff occupied.

Her heart melted as she viewed a sleeping Dawn lovingly held by a dozing adult. He'd strapped the baby to his body using a front carrier. The child seemed surprising comfortable being so close to him. He could still help with the other babies, but Dawn remained quiet and calm as long as she was near him.

Jeff had stopped rocking, and his mouth mimicked the child's. Both were partially opened while their breathing fell into a slow, sleep-related pattern. The picture was priceless. Allison rose from the ground and took Evan with her as she searched for her camera. They'd taken pictures of their field trip to the post office, and she'd even managed to sneak a shot of Jeff's smiley boxers.

Locating her camera, she tiptoed over to Ryan's CEO sitting in the rocker cradling an infant and took a quick picture. Neither man nor child so much as blinked. Allison took a second shot and put the camera away.

Realizing they had to prepare the babies for the parents' arrivals, Allison woke Jeff. With a lazy grin, he got up. They made one last diaper change on all the babies and waited. When all the children had been picked up, both fell into a quiet routine of cleaning up the center.

"Hi, you two."

Allison and Jeff turned toward the center's front door as Elizabeth waltzed in.

"Mom, I've seen you more since Friday than I have in a month."

"I swear I raised you the same way I did your sister, and she turned out to be such a wonderful, obedient child," Elizabeth lectured as she strolled past Jeff.

"Stop comparing me to the saint of the family. I'm never gonna be another Sister Margaret Mary, so get over it. Be happy with me the way I am." He shot a look at Allison. "Go on. Tell her how lovable I am."

Allison crossed her arms before answering. "How would I know?" She hoped neither would notice the heated blush that surely stained her cheeks.

As Jeff grinned, his mother gave a dry comment, "Kindly rephrase your rude comment to me when I walked in."

Jeff dropped his head into his hands and rubbed his forehead. "Mother, why are you here?"

She sniffed. "Father O'Brien wants to meet with us tomorrow night for dinner. Since you never did give Allison that lunch you promised her, I hoped she'd join us. If she'll agree to go with you, of course."

"Why wouldn't she go? The woman adores me. Don't you, Allison?"

"Huh? Did you just ask me something, fellow babysitter?"

"Yeah, well, okay. We don't just babysit here."

"Thank you."

"You're welcome."

Elizabeth said, "Are we all having dinner with the Archbishop or not?"

"I'd love to go, Mrs. Ryan. I'll bring a change of clothes here and meet you wherever we're going."

"Jeff? Will this fit into your busy social life?" His mother quipped.

"No problem. I'll cancel all my dates and pencil this in. I wouldn't want Allison to go without eating."

Allison rolled her eyes at his comment. Dinner with Jeff. Sure, his mother and the Archbishop would be there to buffer their conversations, but could she handle being near him all day and at night too?

"It would be more convenient for you to go in one car. Just a suggestion. Parking downtown near Mama Mia's Tripoli can be difficult. I'm meeting Father O'Brien, and he and I will go together. Meet us there at seven."

Jeff and Allison stared at each other. In a soft tone, she finally offered, "You drive. We'll leave my car here."

"Fine. I'll bring my clothes and change here too."

Elizabeth cleared her throat. "I'll see you tomorrow night. And, Allison? Bring your appetite. Jeff's paying."

Allison grinned. "Sure thing. I can't wait."

They watched as Elizabeth said, "I'll see you later," before she slipped out the door.

After moving the last two cribs to the storage closet in complete silence, Jeff headed out the door in front of her so she could lock up.

"Don't forget your good clothes for dinner," Allison offered. To test his patience and add a teasing note before they parted for the night, she joked, "Maybe you'll wear those smiley shorts?"

Jeff stopped dead in his tracks and spun around to face her. "My good clothes don't have a hole in them, so if you want to see what I'm wearing under my pants, I suggest we make other plans."

"Funny, Jeff. I've already seen your boxers, so you can leave the pants on." A ripple of lust streamed through her as she visualized Jeff in nothing but those smiley shorts. A craving to glimpse what was under them made her heart beat faster, and naughty erotic images flooded her mind.

Jeff walked over closer to her and whispered in her ear, "You can see my smiley shorts anytime. Keep that in mind."

While whistling, he pivoted and jaunted over to his car.

Allison couldn't name the tune he whistled. Maybe it was because her mind was still concentrating on his smiley boxers and what was hidden behind them.

Chapter Seven

On Thursday, an embarrassed Allison arrived a few minutes late to find Jeff casually leaning against the wall, dressed in jeans and a fitted T-shirt. Wrenching her gaze from his muscled chest, she fumbled with her keys in a rush to unlock the door.

"Sorry. I hit some traffic this morning," she offered as an apology.

"I just got here myself."

He followed her inside and asked, "Where can I hang these?"

Allison turned toward him and saw Jeff lift up a hanging clothes bag.

"Just put them in the back of the supply closet. Did you get a good night's sleep?"

"Well-rested and ready for another fun-filled day. Should I be leery of reading the chart? Any more unexpected challenges gonna pop out at me?"

"Every day's a new day. Just go with the flow. What else could I possibly put up there that would surprise you?" Allison teased.

He rubbed his chin in mock concentration. "Mountain climbing? Music lessons? Teaching them to drive?"

"Nope. None of those. I don't know about your mountain climbing or driving skills, but I've heard your off-key singing." She laughed. "Just put on your apron. Today you're Betty Crocker's alter ego. It's Kitchen Day." Allison grinned as she waltzed into the kitchen.

Jeff followed her into the room and asked, "Who'll be here today to help us enjoy cooking?"

"It's Thursday so Alex, Susan, Robert, Maria, and Greg are here in the morning. Michael, Jeremy, Rina, Tina, and Connor come in the afternoon. The ones who didn't come yesterday called in as no-shows again today." She shrugged. "So I guess we'll just have five in the morning and five after noon. You'll need to make out more name tags."

"No babies?"

"Nope. Just preschoolers." Somewhat irritated, Allison observed the smug look on his face. Was he happy because he didn't have to deal with infants or because the class size would be smaller? It certainly would make things easier for him, just like yesterday. Had someone somehow orchestrated the absences?

Don't go getting paranoid. Jeff wouldn't do that. Allison dismissed her niggling doubts and blamed it all on fate. Maybe he was meant to have it easier. Not too much easier, but just enough so he wouldn't quit. Maybe divine intervention controlled their days together, and she was destined to spend the weekend with him.

Surely after his week with her at the center, he'd agree to some type of funding even if he won the dare and his weekend. She'd slipped in a few comments about the rent increase and her vision for a bigger and newer daycare. And she counted on his fair assessment of her request.

She eyed Jeff as he stood by the chart and wrote notes for himself. He took a seat in one of the children's chairs, bending his long frame to fit uncomfortably at a low table. Head lowered, he busied himself at the task of writing out name tags.

There he sat. Jeff, the man she loved. Carefully printing—

Man she loved? Jeff? The words Jeff and love had come together in one sentence again and easily slipped into her head. Could love happen that quickly? She didn't have time to answer the question; she needed to focus on work.

She followed Jeff's movement to the door and watched as he

greeted the children when they walked into the center. Once all the kids had arrived, Allison had them sit in a circle for their morning routine. Each child took a turn giving their speeches on what they'd like to do for the day.

Allison turned toward the formerly dead giant, as Robert had called Jeff upon arrival, before speaking. "I'm Miss Allison. Today I want to help everyone cook lunch."

Jeff gave her a rakish grin, stood, and announced, "I'm Mr. Jeff, and today I want to cook up a storm with Miss Allison in the kitchen."

"Mr. Jeff? Are we making rain?" Robert asked his question with total sincerity.

"No," piped up Alex. "We want snow!"

Shouts for snow filled the room until Jeff raised a finger to his lips in a be-quiet gesture.

"Okay, Mr. Jeff. Explain this one." Allison stifled a laugh.

"We're not cooking up weather. Just food. Maybe Miss Allison will get so hot she'll have to take off her apron."

With a grin tugging at the corners of her mouth, Allison said, "I don't think so, Mr. Jeff. Since you're in charge, you'll be doing the cooking. I'm just gonna sit by and read the recipe for you."

"Mr. Gef? Can I be your helper?" Susan giggled as she rocked back and forth on her bottom.

"Sure. All of you can be helpers. Miss Allison thinks I can't cook, so we'll have to show her we all can."

"You can cook? My Daddy says men don't know how to do that," Greg stated.

"We men have to show the ladies we can do anything they can do, and that includes cooking. Right, guys?"

After getting the kids in the kitchen, Allison watched a nervous Jeff read over the recipe she'd handed him.

"What's a pinch? I don't see a measuring spoon here with that label." Jeff threw his question over his shoulder and quickly pivoted in Allison's direction.

She leaned back against the sink, content to watch him as he stood by the kitchen center island surrounded by five eager-to-help, wiggling bodies.

"Just what it says. Two fingers together. Grab a little bit of salt, and voilá, you have a pinch. Relax. Help them make their pizzas while you make some for the afternoon group."

"Mr. Jeff, how much longer? Isn't it my turn yet?" That came from Robert who jiggled in his seat while poking Alex who was sitting next to him.

"Mr. Jeff, tell Robert to quit it. It's my turn. He always wants to do things when it's my turn. Just like with Barney."

"Do not!"

"Do too!"

"Guys! Settle down. We have some serious cooking to do, and we want the ladies to see we can do this."

Allison moved closer to the kitchen island. "Kids, listen to Mr. Jeff. He's in charge." She noted his sigh of relief and the eager looks on the kid's faces as the arguing ended.

"Thanks, Miss Allison." He gave her a slight nod before turning to grin at the kids.

"Alex, you help me pour the tomato sauce into the bowl. It says six cups. Let's all count while we do this."

Alex shoveled sauce into the measuring cup then dumped it into a mixing bowl. Splatters of red dotted the counter, the child, and Jeff's formerly white apron.

Pushing the sauce aside, Jeff offered Susan the chance to measure out the flour for the pizza dough. Allison rested her elbows on the tiled counter top, determined to get a better view of the chef and apprentices at work. The little girl proved more efficient than her male counterpart but still managed to send flour dust flying in all directions.

"Thanks, Susan." Jeff sneezed. "Robert," he turned to the squirming figure to his right, "you put in the water. Just pour in all of it from the measuring cup."

The child did as told. With one giant shake, he dumped the

liquid into the flour, misting the air with a second haze of flour dust. Allison smiled at the funny but adorable scene unfolding before her. While the children laughed at the floating white cloud, Jeff glanced at her with a brown-eyed warmth she welcomed. After wiping his face free from the white dust, he stretched out his hands toward her. With tender, gentle strokes, he painted flour streaks on her face.

"Didn't think you'd get away that easy, did you, Miss Allison? We wouldn't want you to miss out on all the fun, right, kids?"

Jeff's laughter instigated another rumble of kiddie giggles. After giving Allison a wink, Jeff clapped his hands.

"Okay. Next we have Maria." Jeff started to sing.

Allison's heart melted like softened butter as he belted out an off-key rendition of two lines from a song about a girl named Maria. The tiny girl hunched her shoulders and tried to cover her happy face with her hands.

Jeff continued to break down Allison's defenses. What grown woman could resist a man who made children laugh and smile?

Maria added the baking powder and then stirred the mess in the mixing bowl. Jeff beamed with approval, and the child's eyes lit up.

Damn it. If he did one more blessedly wonderful thing, Allison would have to throw her arms around him. To hell with propriety.

"Greg, my man. You're going last, but you have an important job to do."

A serious look covered the child's face. "I can't cook. I make a mess."

Jeff patted him on the back, leaving a partially white handprint. "Not to worry, pal. Everyone has trouble with things sometimes. You pour in the oil, and I'll help you by stirring."

The supportive nod he gave the hesitant young boy striped Allison's resolve. An irresistible urge to satisfy a dozen sexual fantasies floating through her head tested her composure and willpower.

Jeff cleared his throat. "Okay, now I'll give each of you some dough. Roll it out with your rolling pins. Watch me. See how to do it? Pat it first with your hands then do this."

He demonstrated the technique, and the preschoolers followed suit as best they could. Jeff then had them clean their hands as he put tomato sauce into five smaller cups.

He handed them each a spoon and showed them how to spread the red paste over their dough. Together they sprinkled the cheese on top to finish their pizzas.

"Everyone go and wash up. You did great. I'll bake our pizzas, and we'll eat after you have quiet time on your mats with some books." Jeff gently lifted the handmade pizzas onto a slightly bent cookie sheet.

The kids scurried out of the kitchen, and he placed their masterpieces in the oven. The extra ones for the afternoon group would be relegated to the refrigerator as soon as he finished making them.

Allison sat on a stool at the end of the counter, swinging one leg crossed over the other as she watched the head pizza maker of Ryan's Rugrats busy at work. When he finished, they started to clean up the counter.

She stretched across the counter to grab the used measuring items and got flour dust on her T-shirt. Before she could react, Jeff slipped to her side and swiveled her seat so her body faced him with her back to the door. He caught her leg between both of his as his hand reached out to brush away the white mess on her shirt.

Allison turned her head and checked through the door. The kids had lined up in the far corner of the room and were resting, busily involved in reading their books. She returned her gaze to him, and a wave of lust washed over her.

Jeff's hand roamed slowly from under her chin to a new, more decadent position by the swell of her breast. Allison tingled as his touch became more urgent, molding his hand to the shape of first one breast then the other. Her T-shirt clung to her body, and her nipples beaded.

"Should I stop?" His eyes commanded her gaze, and his gravelly voice held an edge of passionate desire.

"No," her voice came out in a raspy whisper. "No, don't stop. Please."

Fire danced in his eyes, and he shifted closer to her. Her leg remained motionless as Jeff positioned his body so her knee remained between his legs in an intimate position. She swung her knee ever so slowly back and forth and listened to Jeff's sudden intake of breath before he groaned. He fondled her breasts with more urgency.

Allison's breathing quickened as her pulse rampaged faster to keep pace with his heightened inhaling and exhaling shudders.

"Oh, Lord, I want you."

Had she said that aloud? Or, had Jeff?

The timer went off, signaling the pizzas were done. Jeff dropped his head and hands to his sides. She assumed he sought some semblance of control just like she grappled for sanity to take hold of her emotions.

"I guess they're done." He sighed. "Us too. For now. I don't think I can let you seduce me again like that and go back to square one."

Buckets of imaginary ice water doused her scorching body. She stood and brushed past him on her way to the side of the counter.

"Seduction? I could have sworn this was mutual consent." She jammed her hands onto her hips.

"Mr. Gef? I'm hungry. Can we eat now?" Susan raced into the kitchen, effectively halting any comment from Jeff.

Allison cooled her temper and faced the little girl. "Sure, honey. Tell the others to put away their books and mats, go wash your hands again, and sit at the table for lunch." She leveled a no-nonsense glance at Jeff. "We're done here."

"Allison, it was a joke," Jeff mumbled and added a puppy-dog look to his face.

Embarrassed at enjoying his caresses but angry at his stupid remark, she refused to accept his explanation. In a totally unladylike manner, she stuck her tongue out at him and marched from the kitchen.

Jeff served lunch and sat with his charges while half-listening to their chatter. He glanced at the kitchen doorway where Allison stayed ensconced, probably hiding from him and the reality of just how far things had moved.

Shit. What the hell had he been thinking by attempting a foreplay session with her so near the kids? Teasing was one thing and hands-on action heightened sexual desires, but this had been a major slip-up in judgment. It placed their credibility at stake. Why hadn't she stopped him?

He gave himself a mental slap on the head. He was the insane one, trying to blame her for their loss of control. As a very willing participant, he'd helped escalate their mutual passion right along with his sexy vixen.

The look she'd given him when he exited the kitchen with the pizzas could have made Attila the Hun shake in his boots. Her comment of, "Stay out of my space," spoke volumes. Voiced as a stinging comment only he could hear, it had made a definite impact, setting the tone for what he assumed would be the rest of the afternoon.

The differences between Allison and Laura seemed staggering. But he'd misjudged before. He'd given his heart to Laura only to have her tear it apart. She hadn't wanted his love but only what he could provide for her. Laura had demanded and enjoyed expensive gifts, trips, and parties. Once he'd made the connection that her favors were only given in exchange for what she wanted, he'd put her to the ultimate test.

Their planned trip to Bermuda, the one that didn't happen, had pushed her over the edge. He couldn't leave work. She didn't care. Laura wanted what Laura wanted. She'd left without a word and moved in with wealthy playboy Phillip Anderson, someone better suited to her flashy lifestyle.

And then, to top it all off, Jeff had found out about her embezzling record. Although relieved he'd missed more damage from a skilled con artist, it still broke his heart. He'd trusted Laura and survived a sure-to-be disastrous match, but it had given his pride and sense of judging people one hell of a blow.

Could Allison be another Laura, teasing him and creating such a state of sexual frustration because she expected him to give up and do her bidding? Hell would freeze over before he'd blindly walk into another Laura trap.

He shook his head and smiled at the kids as they ate. Maybe Allison actually did want him. Chomping down on a piece of his pizza, Jeff wondered if after Friday they could sort things out, both in business and in a more personal way.

The center meant a lot to her, and he could understand why. Jeff surveyed the room and formulated more metal notes to add to all the ones he'd processed since his first day at Ryan's Rugrats. Her proposed expansion and modernizing the center made sense and surely would benefit his employees. But, now wasn't the time to talk about this. He wanted to be sure Glenn had initiated all the plans they'd discussed before surprising Allison.

Then again, what about their one-on-one relationship? Would she figure she'd gotten what she wanted and exit his life? That thought made it hard for him to swallow his last piece of pizza.

At the end of the day, Allison watched as Jeff trudged his way to the supply closet and retrieved his clothes.

"I really think we should go in our own cars. I don't want to take you out of your way to bring me back here." Allison offered her statement while trying to sound practical.

Jeff stopped his trek out of the room and turned toward her. He held his change of clothes in one hand, resting the other hand on the main door of the center.

"There's no need to take separate cars. That just doesn't make sense for either of us."

"But—"

His glare stifled her reply. "I'm using the men's room down the hall. Why don't we both try to be in a better mood when we leave?" Jeff marched away.

Allison slumped against the nearby table. "Crap," she grumbled. She had good reasons for wanting to put some distance between them. Was he only after her body? An affair? Her nerves caused her to twitch with the admission that he'd made it through yet another day. Only one left to go. He'd been able to prove her wrong so far. If the other kids had been there, it might have been a different story.

A tricky, conniving boss might change his employees' schedules, send them on trips. Pushing aside those suspicious thoughts, Allison grabbed her dress and headed into the center's adult bathroom. Logical reasons to keep their relationship on a professional level filled her head although her body yearned for a much more intimate bond.

They'd ride together. Maybe she'd get a chance to throw in some of her ideas for improving the center. Dinner would be pleasant, and at least two more people would be there to buffer their differences. Her biggest worry could come at five the next night, after the center closed. That's when she might become his for the weekend. Maybe worry wasn't the right word to use. Heat seared her cheeks as she realized that the desire to have Randy Ryan all to herself was all she'd been thinking about since their first meeting. Deep in her heart, she wanted the weekend to happen.

Their ride to dinner was more amiable than she'd hoped as they laughed at a funny news story on the radio. Once they'd parked the car and entered the restaurant, she noted how the hostess addressed Jeff by name and asked them to follow her to a table.

As Allison strolled into the dining room, she spotted Elizabeth seated next to an older, white-haired man dressed in black, complete with a white collar.

"Father O'Brien, this is Allison Minetti." Jeff pulled out a chair for Allison.

After greetings were exchanged, she and Jeff sat. He poured a glass of wine from the bottle sitting on the table and offered it to her before pouring a glass for himself.

"Jeffrey, I understand you've been working at a daycare facility this week. How's that going?" Father O'Brien queried with a look of interest.

Jeff arched an eyebrow as he glanced from Father O'Brien to Allison before answering. "Fine. Actually, it wasn't as difficult as I thought it would be. Certainly surprised a lot of people."

"My, yes. I never knew you had it in you," Elizabeth stated.

"Thanks for your support, Mother." Jeff lifted his glass and tasted his wine.

"Uh, Allison. How do you think Jeffrey is doing?" Father O'Brien asked.

"Fine, but he didn't have to deal with as many children as we normally have, so that made it much easier for him." Her still-suspicious comment found its target.

Jeff placed his glass on the table and stared at her. "I spent two days with ten kids. It's not my fault only five came yesterday and today."

Elizabeth clanked her water glass down on her silverware, sloshing water onto the table.

A tinge of annoyance at his daycare-handling-ease comment swept through Allison. Counting to ten didn't help much because it reminded her of the ten kids that should have been at the center the last two days to make his job harder. Jeff tried to portray his foray as director for the center as nothing more than something he encountered every day in his usual corporate dealings.

Temptation urged her to gain everyone's attention and tell her audience just how good he managed in his new position. "Yes. He did spend Monday and Tuesday with all the kids."

"Damn right," Jeff said.

Allison itched to wipe away the smug look on his face. "And, I'd love to tell you all about it. Would you like to hear about the child throwing up on him, the little boy who kicked him in the shins, or about his dead giant acting debut?

"My favorite has to be his sexy red and purple smiley face shorts and the wonderful picture a four-year-old made of them for him to hang on the wall. I have tons of stories." Her voice had taken on a sing-song tone.

Elizabeth and Father O'Brien looked at each other, then at her. Allison felt a stinging heat creep up her face.

Jeff's hand reached under the table and tenderly squeezed her thigh. She jumped, adding to her embarrassment. His hand continued making lazy circles by her knee.

"You tell mine, I'll tell yours."

Father O'Brien cleared his throat. "Uh, Jeffrey, that music sounds wonderful. Your mother and I need to discuss the charity ball coming up, so why don't you take Allison for a spin on the dance floor? Don't mind us old folks. Enjoy the music."

"Oh, that's all right. We don't have to—" Allison got no further.

"What she means to say is what a great suggestion. Excuse us, please. Allison?" Jeff stood and offered his hand.

She had no alternative but to take it and have him lead her away from their table. "Why did you do that?"

"Partially because I didn't want you to start playing Show and Tell back there. And don't think for one minute I wouldn't come across with stories about you."

"Me? What could you possibly say?" Allison tried to yank free from his grasp.

"Forgetful, aren't we? Let's see. You kissed me many, many times, sat on my lap and danced around, stroked your knee on my—"

"Stop right there. Some of those things happened away from the center."

Jeff tugged her tightly in his embrace. In a husky tone he challenged, "But not all. That knee thing you did today at the center? Rubbing me like that had me aroused for hours."

Were they fighting or friends again? He'd turned their verbal combat into erotic fantasies, transforming her defensive stand into mush.

"We sure do an awful lot of arguing." Her body relaxed as tension evaporated between them and electricity sparked instead.

Jeff stroked her forehead with his chin. Loving, tender touches given with a slight scratch from his five o'clock shadow caused Allison's blood to pump faster. Raw, amorous-filled visions of how they could spend the weekend danced in her head.

She conceded defeat. He'd make it through the week. She'd be with him all weekend. They'd do whatever came naturally. Her body wanted him. They'd make love. And, it would be great.

"No more fighting tonight, okay? Save that for tomorrow when I get you all to myself," he suggested in a whispered tone.

Allison nodded while she burned with need and passionate eagerness. She welcomed the flirting banter she and Jeff employed while he held her close and they danced. Snuggled up tightly against his chest, she could sense the rhythm of his heartbeat and knew hers matched his.

The rest of their evening fell into a smooth and comfortable pattern. Dancing was mingled with sitting, eating, and interesting chatter at their table. Allison enjoyed talking to Father O'Brien, and both he and Elizabeth embarrassed Jeff a few times with stories of his youthful adventures.

Jeff held her hand as they walked to his car for their ride back to the center. They talked about his childhood stories, giving Jeff a chance to add his side to every naughty tale his mother had mentioned at dinner. Allison joined in his laughter and memorized his stories for future reference.

When he parked the car, she offered with a sincere smile, "Thanks for driving me back." Allison reached for the handle to open the door.

"Please wait. Let me get out first." The tired plea in his voice gave her no choice.

He walked around the car and opened her door. His body shifted from one side to the other as if seeking a comfortable position.

"Thank you." Allison's eyes sought his face. In the moonlight and with the street light overhead, she couldn't help but notice the pale countenance he presented. "Are you okay?"

"Yeah. Just tired, and my stomach's dancing a bit. Maybe it was that fourth pizza I had today." His attempt at a grin still didn't cover his obvious discomfort as he winced.

Allison put her hand on his forehead. "You're a bit hot. Maybe you're coming down with something."

Jeff took her wrist and brought her hand to his lips where he feathered a delicate kiss.

"I'll be fine. All I need is something to settle the tomato sauce fighting with that spicy Béarnaise from my steak, and I'll sleep like a baby."

She noted the strange look on his face. His brow furrowed, and his hand dropped hers to pat his stomach. He inhaled, let out a whoosh, and then checked his watch.

"I guess it's getting late. See you tomorrow." His hand cupped her chin. "Don't forget your suitcase. It won't be on your chart, but tomorrow's Consequence Day."

Chapter Eight

Allison heard Jeff coming before he strolled into the center with a lazy swagger to his step. He whistled the same song some cartoon characters sang as they merrily toddled off to work. And he was more on-key than his singing voice had demonstrated.

"Good morning, Miss Allison. My, don't you look sweet and bubbly today."

"Hello yourself. You look better today. Take lots of vitamins? Where's your gallon of java? You know," she raised an eyebrow at him, "the dare's not over until five. You still might not make it."

"Oh, no." Jeff shook his head as he laughed. "You won't burst my balloon so easily." He took a quick turn around the room, even checking out the closets and bathrooms. Returning to where she worked on sorting paints, he inquired, "So? Where's your suitcase? Or did you decide to tempt fate, and eventually me, by not bringing anything?"

"My stuff's in the car." She prayed her voice sounded confident and didn't betray the nerve-wracking and knotted stomach jitters rampaging inside her. "That way, I won't have far to carry it when I go home tonight and bring it inside after you give up."

Jeff wiggled his eyebrows before saying in a confident tone, "Never happen," then he zeroed in on the day's chart.

"Yeah, well, just read away, Mr. CEO. Lots on the agenda for today." *Damn. I sound like a pouting three-year-old.*

A momentary pang of guilt collided with sympathy for him as she noticed him rubbing his side. Was he still not feeling well?

"Swim Day?" His voice boomed through the almost empty room. Shifting his gaze toward Allison, he added, "Did you sneak something special into the schedule?"

Affronted, she bit back, "No. The kids take lessons at the community center every other week. I vary the day to give them all a chance to swim, although we don't do Tuesdays. Too many babies to handle.

"While the three older kids take their lesson, I usually jump in with the infants one at a time. Usually the parent with me keeps an eye on the remaining little one. You just lucked out today and get to go."

With a sheepish grin and contrite tenor to his voice, Jeff offered an apology. "Sorry about that. Lucky thing I have a bathing suit stashed in my suitcase." He winked at her. "Figured you might like to try drowning me in the hotel's pool or Jacuzzi."

Allison sighed. "Promises, promises. I hadn't planned on you doing water aerobics, but since this is your last day as director you should be handling this."

"Me? In the water with a baby? I barely manage them on dry land."

Smirking, Allison challenged, "What happened to your anything-you-can-do attitude? Are you backing down?"

Jeff stretched and rubbed his side again. "Nope. I'll jump in."

"Are you sure you're okay?"

"Yeah. I'm fine. They do wear diapers, don't they?"

"Yep. Special ones for water use."

"You're doing this just because you want to see me in my bathing suit. Admit it, Miss Allison." He shook a finger at her. "Actually, never mind. It's enough knowing you know that I know. I'm flattered."

She leaned against a table and folded her arms in front of her. "Oh, absolutely," she teased. "Nothing else has crossed my mind day and night since we've met but how virile you must look in a bathing suit. I've lost sleep all week thinking about it."

"You're beautiful when you're irritated at me. Sarcasm brings out a fiery look in your sexy blue eyes that I can't ignore." He headed for the door as his first rugrat ran in.

Allison mumbled, "Let's see how your day goes," but he was already out of range and didn't hear.

The plague of absences haunted the center yet another day. The same five kids, the ones she'd hoped would return to round out the ten she had counted on, wouldn't be there. The calls came just as they had on Wednesday and Thursday. Allison once again had phoned the volunteer parents informing them their presence wouldn't be necessary.

She glanced at a busy Jeff as he juggled two infants on his lap and sat on the carpet chatting with the three preschoolers. Giggles floated through the air. She loved the way he attempted to look interested in whatever the kids rambled on about. He'd be a great father.

And, she'd be at a hotel with him all weekend.

Jeff surveyed the pool's surroundings with its heated, clammy atmosphere. "Nice place."

"You stay here with Rose and Brian. I'll go bring Susan, Connor, and Amy over to their class," Allison said.

With the two infants in a double stroller, Jeff found a seat in a bleacher area off to the side of the pool. The babies made tiny noises but nothing he deemed worrisome. From his position, he viewed Allison and her charges as they meandered to where three swimming instructors stood with three other children.

Wiping his brow, Jeff noted how uncomfortably warm he felt. The indoor pool area almost misted with humidity. He unbuttoned his shirt, hoping for relief. His years as a high school and college quarterback should have conditioned him to ignore the heat, but maybe he'd been off a playing field too long.

Allison's return jolted him. "They're all set. Now for the babies."

"Who goes first? Rose or Brian? What am I supposed to be doing once we jump in?"

"You can jump in all by yourself. I'll hand Rose to you. Bob up and down with her, spin her around, and help her splash. Do fun stuff. We try to get them to be at ease in the water so they're not afraid."

Jeff nodded and stood to remove his clothes. "Are you gonna watch me and make sure I don't drown?"

As if considering his suggestion, Allison stated, "Absolutely. You did say I could drown you myself, didn't you? I wouldn't want you to take that little pleasure away from me."

Screams of "Mr. Gef," "Mr. Jeff," and "Miss Allison" caught their attention. The three students were happily wading in the low end of the pool and calling out for some recognition.

"Coming!" Allison yelled back. "I'll wheel this over to that side so I can watch the kids. You jump in and swim over to me, and then I'll lower Rose in."

"Anything you say."

⁂

Allison couldn't help staring at the grown man gliding through the water holding up a wiggling child. He had crooned encouraging words to Rose when the infant first got water on her face and looked ready to wail.

Playing football sure had toned up his physique, even if it had been years since Jeff had played. He'd told her about his college days and how he now worked out occasionally at the gym.

Allison got enough exercise chasing kids all day. She had no need, energy, or time for anything else. Although, she'd welcome the opportunity to go dancing now and then but only with the right partner. That kind of exercise would be more enjoyable than simply jogging or running on a treadmill. And she already knew

Jeff could dance. Maybe throwing that in during her upcoming weekend would help fill the time they'd spend together. The hotel would surely offer a music and dancing spot, or they could always find a club downtown.

Jeff waded over to her and gently lifted a wiggling Rose out of the water. Allison wrapped the child in a towel, and Jeff bobbed up and down, sloshing water over the edge of the pool.

"Why don't you swim a few laps?" she suggested. "Brian's snoozing, so we'll give him a few more minutes to rest. I'll watch them."

"Thanks. I'd like to get some kinks out. I'm a little achy from lack of exercise."

"No problem. Go for it."

His body sliced through the water as he did laps back and forth in front of Allison. His frame illustrated the style and grace of any accomplished swimmer. Smooth ripples cascaded from his every well-timed movement. Allison longed to caress the wet muscled areas of his arms and legs that tightened and relaxed with every stroke.

Jeff swam over to her, flicking droplets of water her way. "Wanna join me?"

Laughing, she answered, "Sorry. Don't have my suit with me. But when we come back this afternoon, I'll give you a break and take a turn with the babies."

His glance traveled to the preschoolers, marching near the pool's steps. "Do I have time to help my mini-people over there?"

"Sure. Come get Brian in five minutes. I'll wake him and get him ready for you."

Jeff yelled out, "Hey, rugrats! Wait for me. I wanna dance in the water too!"

As he swam toward the happy threesome, Allison scored another plus for him on her list of his good and bad points. The positive side kept out-scoring the negatives. How could anyone not love a man who jumped up and down in the water with preschoolers and seemed to have as much fun as they did?

When they returned to the pool with the afternoon group, it was Allison's turn to hop in with the babies. She slid out of her pants and folded them neatly on the bench. Then she pulled off her T-shirt and stacked it on top of her jeans.

"Nice suit. Buy it at Bikinis-R-Us?"

Rolling her eyes, Allison reached out to Jeff and gave him a playful shove. "This is a tankini. I don't look good in bikinis."

He let his eyes roam from the top of her head to the bottom of her legs. Heat soared through her system each second his full attention was zeroed in on her.

"Well, Miss Allison, I definitely like what I see. You're a beautiful, desirable woman. I'm anxious to spend time with you in a Jacuzzi. Just the two of us. Maybe without suits, if I can convince you to throw caution to the wind and dive in with me." He winked. "Feeling frisky?"

"Shhh. Someone might hear you."

Jeff made an obvious gesture of surveying the nearby area. "Everyone's at that end of the pool. Jesse and Ruth here," he pointed to the two afternoon infants waiting for their water sessions, "well, I don't think they'll talk."

"It doesn't matter. Please don't do that. You make me uncomfortable."

"Sorry." He reached out and covered her hands with his. "That's the last thing I want to do. But you are beautiful, and I am looking forward to this weekend."

"So am I." She'd said it aloud, told him what bubbled inside her: desire to spend time alone together and to take their relationship in whatever direction it led.

Passion blazed in his eyes. "Go jump in. I need time to breathe normally instead of conjuring up wild images of us later tonight. I'll hand you Jesse and then take Ruth over to the other side to watch the trio take their lesson."

Allison did as told. Willing her thoughts to concentrate on water play with infants, she pushed erotic expectations of what could develop that evening far back in her mind. *Kids now, grown-up play later.*

Anything You Can Do

At four o'clock, the kids were resting back at the center. Allison had been amazed that Jeff had made it through two swim sessions although he'd looked more tired than she'd imagined. She checked the two infants sleeping peacefully in their cribs and then tiptoed over and joined Jeff, Mary-Ellen, Marcus, and Michael at story-time.

"Okay M, M, and M. You guys make me think of my favorite candy. Let's read one story than settle back on our mats." Jeff tousled Michael's hair and then tickled the other two.

"How about this book?" Allison handed Jeff a story about kids and teddy bears.

"Sure, Miss Allison. Should we read this one, guys?"

The tykes agreed, and Jeff read the story supplying different voices for the various characters. Yawning, he put the book away as the kids settled down.

"Do you mind if I rest with them? Or is there anything I need to do?" Jeff asked.

"Go ahead. I'm just gonna sit here," she replied keeping her seat on the rocking chair. "We really don't have anything else to do except get them up and ready fifteen minutes before their parents come."

Allison grinned as she witnessed the kids vying to snuggle next to a reclining Jeff. Two laid their tiny heads on his chest, his arms surrounding them. Mary-Ellen couldn't find a spot near him, so she walked over to Allison and sat on her lap.

This feels good. Both of us sharing love with kids. Allison rocked the drowsy child in her arms, listening to the almost quiet sounds in the room. The infants were already asleep, and Marcus and Michael with their eyes closed laid firmly planted next to their protector.

Jeff looked natural reclining on kiddie mats and holding his charges. Only an occasional snoring sound broke through the silent room, a sign that he napped just like the preschoolers.

Do I love him?

The words echoed in Allison's head, bouncing back and forth and breaking any barriers her mind attempted to erect. Although they'd only known each other a short time, he'd managed to stir the passion and lust inside her to new heights, creating a desire and need for him. Maybe their whole encounter had been orchestrated by the heavens above. To hell with the consequences. She wanted him, he wanted her, and they would make incredible love together.

Allison sighed, causing the sleeping Mary-Ellen to change position on her lap. She glanced at the clock and began a countdown to their affair. At the end of the day, Allison waited for Jeff. He'd won fair and square, but maybe she had too.

"You still look tired," she said as she observed his sluggish appearance.

"Yeah, maybe I am. Two trips to that humid pool area did a number on me. I'll be okay once we get to the hotel." He reached for her and caressed her cheek with his knuckles. "I won't hold you to this, you know."

Full of desire and need, she stated, "I want to go."

A desperate craving to be held in his arms again while enjoying more passionate kisses and loving caresses, burned through her.

"Great." He brushed her lips with his. "I want this to happen too."

"Jeff, after being here a week, is there any chance you'd still consider my request for funding? I'll understand if you say no."

Allison wanted their weekend to be about them, not about the center or hinging on any "I won, you lost" stipulations. If he could satisfy her one concern by just agreeing to think about her suggestions, she'd banish all her daycare worries and spend their time concentrating on what they both wanted.

Jeff eyed her with caution, hoping Allison wouldn't gauge their time spent together on whether or not she got her way. Was that her motive in asking him about his decision? Hell, he'd decided to become her business partner after his first day. He realized more help, paid help, was needed. And her major plan for renovating and expanding the program displayed insight and a keen sense of business on her part. She wanted to offer more of his employees an opportunity for childcare services, and anything that would help his workers sounded like a good plan.

But for their weekend, he wanted her to be with him because she shared the same mutual hunger he felt for her. Maintaining his balance on this tightrope of wants, needs, and desires would take more than diplomacy. He needed courage to stand resolute. He wouldn't have another Laura on his hands, in his bed, and in his heart.

Hesitating to form the words in a noncommittal sentence, he finally offered, "Being here all week with you and the rugrats has been an eye-opener for me. Can we have our weekend and deal with this next week after I get back from my trip?" He prayed she'd give a convincing response, one he'd bank on coming from her heart.

A bright smile greeted him. "Sure, I understand. Let's go."

Jeff couldn't judge her comment or read her body language. He only heard the tone he wanted to hear and saw an alluring temptress weaving her spell. That's what he hoped for.

"See you there."

Jeff hopped in his Mercedes and waited for Allison to start her Honda. Exhausted, he was grateful that the drive to the hotel would be a short one.

Once at the hotel and registered, he handed Allison her door key and suggested she check her room. Pleasing her became his number one priority. "We share a connecting door so just pop in after you make sure the room is okay for you."

It didn't take long for Allison, bubbling with enthusiasm, to sweep into his room. "My room is beautiful. I can't believe the view I have from up here. Yours must be the same."

"Yep. These are the best suites. I stay here once in a while just so I can enjoy seeing the city at night. Are you unpacked?"

"Not yet. I had to come and thank you. The flowers are lovely."

She smiled, and her eyes sparkled.

He rocked on his heels. "I figured you deserved something for letting me sleep this afternoon. I left you covering the center while I snoozed."

"You were tired, and the kids slept right along with you. Anyway, I managed to get some great blackmail shots of you napping with two preschoolers tucked in next to your body. Maybe I'll have one made up for Christmas cards and send them to everyone in your company."

Jeff lowered his head and rocked it from side to side. "Honey, that'll cost you a fortune. I have over three hundred employees. And what could you possibly hope to get by blackmailing me? Singing lessons? Cooking tips? All the skills I displayed this week?"

Rubbing her chin, Allison answered, "Hmm. None of those came to mind before you mentioned them. But, I would like to know the secret you shared with Robert on Monday. It's been bugging me all week."

Jeff laughed. "That's it? All I have to do is tell you what words of wisdom I imparted to Robert? Boy, that's easy."

"I never said that would do it. Maybe that's just part of my plan. Get you to tell me one thing per picture. I took six this week, by the way."

Jeff stopped midway in his trek to the closet where he'd gone to hang his jacket. "Pretty busy with that camera. Do you already have five other ransoms figured out for the rest of the photos, or are you gonna make them up as you go along?"

With a saucy look, she quipped, "Not telling. I can't give away all my secrets. Strategy is very important when blackmailing someone."

"Serves me right for getting involved with a female over the age of four."

"Little girls grow up and learn how to deal with men," Allison teased.

"I know. And the grown-up versions are much more enticing.

Go unpack, blackmailing woman. I'll tell you about my friend Robert at dinner in," he checked his watch, "thirty minutes. We have reservations at the American Restaurant."

Once unpacked, they went through the lobby to a cab parked outside. Jeff figured that it would be easier to use cabs than his car during their stay. Trying to find a parking spot in the city, especially at night, would be difficult.

He noticed Allison's look of surprise once inside the restaurant, and it pleased him knowing he could make things special for her. They were led to a table, took their seats, and placed their wine order.

Allison whispered across to him, "This place is so elegant. I've never been here before."

"We would've had lunch at another place like this last week if you hadn't broken my elevator."

She laughed. "Are you trying to test my bad side?"

Reaching across the table, Jeff took her hand, brought it up to his lips, and kissed her fingertips. "I promise to be good. Although, if I get to caress your hand to apologize, I may have to rethink my strategy."

"Don't get your hopes up. I'm more of a pacifist than a fighter. Anyway, for picture number one, what did you say to Robert?"

Chapter Nine

Allison noted the innocent look in his eyes as Jeff answered, "I told him that as men we had to stick together and not upset the females. We didn't want Miss Allison to cry if we weren't buddies."

"Those were your words of wisdom?"

Jeff shrugged. "Hey, it worked, didn't it? He became my best friend most of the time, except, of course, for Susan, my pint-size admirer."

"You mean the youngest female to propose to you?"

"Maybe I should wait twenty years and take her up on her offer."

"You'd be too old for her," Allison teased.

"Ah, yes." He gave a fake sigh. "But she'd be young enough for me," Jeff quipped and added a wink.

Their eyes connected in a stare of shared desire, and a momentary silence hung between them. Allison blocked out the clattering of silverware, the tinkling of glasses, and the chatter of other patrons sprinkled throughout the room.

They'd have dinner and let passion take over back at the hotel. She trembled slightly with a lusty craving to satisfy her need for Jeff.

"Why don't we order? You got one ransom out of me so far. I'm sure you'll take this opportunity to dream up more demands in exchange for the pictures while we eat."

"I already have something in mind," Allison retaliated.

Jeff arched his eyebrows and pulled a lopsided grin to one side of his mouth. "Those wheels inside your head never stop, do they? Okay. What is it?"

Feigning interest on the menu, she offered, "Hmm? Oh, I'll have stuffed mushrooms, Veal Marsala, Caesar salad, and a baked potato. Another glass of wine with dinner would be fine."

"Right. Now about your blackmail request for picture number two?"

Allison leaned slightly over the table and in a hushed whisper replied, "Tell me all about Randy Ryan at college."

Narrowing his eyes, he asked, "You're sure you want to hear this?"

She sat back and realized his comment had piqued her curiosity even further. "Absolutely. I need to know all the fascinating details."

Jeff sipped at his wine, cleared his throat, and uttered, "Here goes. The rise and fall of Randy Ryan."

During dinner, she listened with rapt attention as he began to entertain her with stories of his past involving his well-earned nickname.

"You didn't." Allison almost choked on her wine after listening to one of Jeff's exploits at school.

With a shrug, he offered an excuse. "Hey, I was young and horny, and she threw herself at me."

"A professor's wife? Didn't either of you worry about being caught?"

Jeff creased his brow as if deep in thought. "I was too stupid to care. Hell, I had rampaging hormones flowing through my body, and sex was all I thought about. After my studies, of course."

"Oh, sure. After your studies," Allison remarked sarcastically.

"Theresa had a long list of students she chased. Her husband turned a blind eye to her affairs." Jeff shook his head. "Alas, I was just one of many admirers enjoying her lessons in lovemaking."

A twinge of jealousy prickled Allison's senses. Had he truly enjoyed all an experienced trooper like the professor's wife gave so freely and apparently with expertise? Allison debated how she'd fare in comparison when they finally made it to bed.

"Shame on you. So far, you've had an older woman chase you and a younger one offer a marriage proposal. Don't women my age interest you?" Allison's question came out in a teasing tone.

"You do."

Her heart rate jumped as anticipation and yearning sped through her body. "Now what?" she asked, with desire edging her questions.

Tossing his napkin on the table, Jeff burned a look at her. "Let's go back to the hotel."

"No dessert?" Her eyes remained riveted on his.

In a low, husky tone, he whispered, "All I want is you."

Busy with her own thoughts, Allison realized that other than offering her smiles with looks of lust, Jeff had remained quiet during their cab ride to their hotel. Her desire heightened to a frenzied state, and she anticipated what the next giant step in their relationship would bring.

As they exited the elevator onto their floor, he broke the silence hanging between them. "Your room or mine?"

Unashamed to display her eagerness as heat soared through her, she said, "I'll be right over. I just need to grab a few things."

Allison entered her suite and carefully closed the door behind her. Leaning against it, she tilted her head to rest it on the rich, mahogany wood. With her eyes closed, she smiled to herself. The strong, gentle, caring type of man she'd always hungered for waited on the other side of their connecting door. He'd shown nothing but warmth and kindness with the kids, a necessary quality to add to her list of attributes for eligible men allowed in her life.

Opening her eyes, she stared into the massive room, one she'd never been accustomed to occupying. The room would be a fleeting pleasure she'd enjoy. Maybe like Jeff. How long would he be in her life?

Michael had given her all the right words and signs that he'd wanted her and that they'd have a future together. He'd listened to her wants and needs and agreed with her suggestion to remove their names from the upcoming promotion search for a new office opening in New York. Allison had detailed how their happiness with each other and being located mid-country kept them closer to family and friends. Ultimately, she had worried hurt feelings could ruin their relationship if one of them got the promotion and the other moved anyway without a job.

Michael had kissed her, praising her for her insightful and honest appraisal of their situation. He'd assured her she'd expressed exactly how he'd felt, so they agreed to stay put in Kansas City. To celebrate their decision and advance their relationship to a higher level, they'd spent a weekend in Branson, Missouri. She'd trusted him completely with her heart.

Two weeks later, Michael announced he'd gotten the promotion and would leave immediately. He invited her to join him in New York after giving him a few months to get settled into his new surroundings. She'd offered her congratulations as her heart hit rock bottom. He'd used her trust and love and shattered her dreams. With her head held high, she had declined his offer.

Jeff couldn't be like him. Their next step didn't involve any underlying subterfuges on his part to win or to get his way. He wouldn't take her trusting heart and move on. Right? Banishing those doubts out of her head, Allison entered the bathroom and grabbed a flimsy pink silk teddie. She figured stripping in front of him would heighten her pleasure, as well as his.

Jeff prayed Allison would decide to come because she wanted to be with him and not because she wanted something. He dimmed the lights in the main room and added some soft music from a radio station to set the mood. He ordered champagne and fresh strawberries, a worthy substitute for the dessert they hadn't had at the restaurant.

"I'm here." Her voice came as a whisper, mellow and calm like the soothing music filtering through the air.

Jeff captured the image of her standing in the doorway, half in, half out, as if seeking permission to come forward. Or, keeping her distance as if rethinking this big step between them.

"I've ordered dessert. Should be here in five minutes. Since I rushed you out of the restaurant, I thought we'd enjoy something here."

Allison bit her bottom lip—the one Jeff longed to kiss endlessly as soon as she gave him a signal. He didn't want to rush her. They had all night. All weekend. Besides, anticipation was part of foreplay, and it aroused him to delightful levels. His whole week with her had bordered on being one huge adventure in foreplay, touching, teasing, tasting, and approaching that brink but never quite getting over the edge. Tonight would be different. They'd jump together.

"That sounds wonderful." Allison sauntered into the room, swinging some piece of pink fabric.

"Are you going to change into that now?" He wanted to beg, but thought it better to give her control of their timing.

"After dessert. Let's try out that Jacuzzi first."

He caught a blush creeping up her cheeks, boiling the blood in his veins. A shaky sigh whooshed from his body, one completed with his heart beating an overtime rhythm as his senses soared. "Really?"

"Of course." She gave him a saucy look. "You did promise I could drown you. I can't do that unless you're in there with me."

The minx rattled his cage, stoked his fire, and pushed all his buttons. "I'm all yours."

A knock on the door broke the sexual tension. Jeff answered it, and a waiter wheeled in a cart loaded with a champagne bucket and strawberries. Jeff tipped the man and closed the door behind him after he left the room. He asked, "Where shall we have these?"

"In there." She pointed to the bathroom. "We can enjoy them while we soak."

With a wiggle of her hips, she sashayed from his main suite room. Jeff grabbed the cart handle and followed after her.

Allison's stomach did flips as she entered the bathroom. The huge space could easily swallow her apartment living room. The toilet and shower areas hid behind separate doors, leaving an enormous Jacuzzi as the focal point. She turned on the faucets, touching the water to gauge the temperature. Without saying a word, Jeff handed her a packet of bubble bath from the basket on the sink counter.

Once the water began to bubble with fresh-scented foam, she turned toward him and started to disrobe. Her shoes went first, and then she reached up one leg and pulled down a thigh-high stocking.

"Need any help?" he offered in a husky voice.

"Why don't you pour that champagne? I'm ready for some."

He cleared his throat, said, "Of course," and turned to uncork the bottle. Aiming it away from her, he popped it open.

Allison continued undressing, her hands shaking with nervous jitters in her no-turning-back decision to strip for him. She relished the lusty look blazing in his eyes as he watched her striptease. She slid her slip down her legs, and it puddled on the floor. Then she turned her back to him but glanced over her shoulder.

"I do need your help. Unzip me, please?" Her request wasn't really a question, but more of a softly spoken command.

Jeff finished pouring two fluted glasses with sparkling pale liquid and set them down near the tub's edge. He stepped over to where she stood and raised his hands to her zipper.

"This isn't a trick to throw me in right now and drown me, is it?"

Reaching behind her to caress his face with her hand, she replied, "Plenty of time for that later."

A groan escaped from his lips. He lowered her zipper, and she delighted in the feathery kisses he placed on her back as he exposed her skin. The kisses ended where the zipper did, past her waist and just shy of her thong.

"Thank you." She stepped away, tugged the dress off her shoulders, and let it fall. Allison pivoted to face him, wearing only a white lace thong and a sheer bra. Her beaded nipples, already aroused, strained the delicate material.

Jeff tore at his clothing and shed his shoes, socks, and jacket quicker than she expected. When he began unbuttoning his shirt, Allison asked, "Can I help?"

His hands stilled. She started at the top button, pushing it easily through the first hole. Her fingertips skipped down his shirtfront. Every loosened button produced a sharp intake of breath from him. Easing the shirt off his broad shoulders, she grazed his skin with her fingernails and worked the material down his arms.

"Thanks." His eyes smoldered with desire.

Inspired by her sense of power, Allison issued her order, "Take off your pants."

She picked up a glass of champagne and took tiny sips of it while her eyes followed his motions. Jeff unbuckled his belt and glided it out of the loops before he unzipped his pants and dropped them to the floor. After gulping the last drop from her glass, Allison's gaze focused on the bulge in his shorts.

"Your turn," he said in a tone edged with desire. "I'll have some champagne while you remove the rest of your things."

Straightening her spine, she reached behind her and undid the bra. The nylon garment slipped from her body and allowed her breasts to bounce free.

Jeff drifted over to her, dipped his finger into his glass, and placed a drop of the liquid on one of her nipples. Then he lowered his mouth to lick it off. Shivering waves cascaded through her body as he laved the sensitive spot. He fingered another drop onto her other nipple, and his mouth lavished the same attention he'd shown the first breast.

Allison ached for more erotic, carnal touches. In a husky voice she didn't recognize as her own, she suggested, "Let's both finish undressing together."

Jeff's boxers hit the ground at the same time as her thong, and moistness pooled between her legs. She strolled over the tub's edge and lowered herself in, causing the water to shimmer with waves. Bubbles tickled her breasts, already sensitive with desire. He joined her, sitting opposite from where she sat. Reaching over, he handed her another glass of champagne.

"Here's to our night together. And our weekend. If you don't drown me, that is." He grinned and then took a sip from his glass.

Allison threw her head back and chugged her drink, placing the glass on the tub's tiled shelf. She took some strawberries and inched her body up along his legs to his knees. Taking one berry in her hand, she offered it to him.

Jeff bit into it, his eyes never straying from her face. Allison took a second berry and held it by her mouth, licking and sucking on it in slow, erotic nibbles.

"Come and get this," he suggested in a seductive whisper. He placed a strawberry halfway in his mouth.

She eased up his legs to his lap, ready and eager to share his offering. Allison's mouth inched closer to his, and her pulse quickened. She nipped at the strawberry in tiny bites. Jeff's hands crept up her thighs to her hips. He clutched her firmly against his body so the length of his arousal pressed against her. His hand roamed the fleshy parts of her rear end as he squeezed and caressed both cheeks. Moans of delight escaped from her lips, and she sucked in the remaining part of the berry, chewing and then swallowing it. She licked at the juice from the fruit that moistened her lips.

"Don't. Let me do that," he begged. His tongue darted out, caressing her lips.

With her eyes shut tight, Allison savored the experience. Sounds of the water rippling around them added to the crackling noise the bubbles made as they dissipated. She inched her hands along his chest to his nipples and rubbed them into tight orbs.

Jeff groaned. "I want you on me and me inside you. Tell me this is what you want too." His plea asked the ultimate question.

Allison's breathing came in short rasps. She wanted it all, just as he'd said, and it would be heaven. But a necessary alarm bell dinged in her head, jolting her to one last stab at reality. Her head dipped forward, and she angled her arms around his shoulders. Raising her face to view the fire in his eyes, she uttered, "We can't."

Jeff tensed, his body stilled, and his breathing came in gulps.

"Not in here. We need protection."

His body relaxed. "I'm sorry. You're right. Should we move to the bed?"

Allison slid down his legs, thrilled to hear his gasps for air as she moved. She prepared to push herself up and out of the tub when his hands caught hers.

"Wait. I have a better idea."

Filled with curiosity and panting like a seductress more than ready to take on an entire football team, she relaxed her arms and slipped back into the lukewarm water.

"Why don't you drain the tub almost all the way and stay put. I'll be right back."

More than willing to do his bidding, Allison scooted back to the end of the tub and unstopped the drain. She watched with hunger as Jeff stepped out, dripping water on the tiled floor. He dried himself off and then grabbed his pants. After rummaging around in one pocket, he took out a condom and opened it. Before placing it over his erection, he turned to her and gave her the sexiest, seductive smile she'd ever received.

"Can I help you do that?" Had she uttered those urgent words?

His smile grew wider. "Honey, if you so much as lay a finger on me right now, we'll never get to the fun part."

He encased himself and returned to the tub. When most of

the water had disappeared, he instructed her to plug the drain and offered his hand to Allison. "If you stand up, I'll dry you off before we settle back in the tub."

She stepped out of the tub and stood naked before him. He dried her front and brushed the cottony material teasingly over her breasts.

"Turn around."

She did as told, and he blotted the water still on her back before guiding the towel to her buttocks.

"Face me and spread your legs."

Allison turned, and her knees almost buckled when she saw Jeff kneeling in front of her. She placed her hands on his shoulders and parted her legs. His eyes smoldered with heat and passion as he gazed at her. With tenderness, he took the towel and gently brushed the center of her female lust. The soft fabric sent shivers of pleasure racing along her body. She craved to feel the length of him inside her.

"Now, Jeff. I can't wait anymore," she begged.

Her body temperature soared as he sank into the tub. Jeff reclined in the shallow water, offering her a better view of his shaft. His hand reached for hers, and he helped her step back into the Jacuzzi.

With his hands planted on her hips for support, she slowly lowered her body. Slick with wanton readiness, she glided onto him. Allison's heart raced as she curled her legs around him. She grinned with amused satisfaction at how wonderfully they fit together.

They began the dance of lovers. Each thrust lifted them higher, driving them toward ecstasy. Each push he made caused tiny splashing sounds as the water tickled her skin. Jeff reached down to stimulate her. Her body burned with desire for the intense throes of climax. Wave after wave of passion erupted, bringing her to the ultimate joy of sexual satisfaction. Spent and panting heavily, Allison matched his rapid breathing.

"Honey, thank you. I knew the first time you did your lap dance on me, I needed you back here in this very spot for real." He kissed her nose.

"You're not too bad yourself. I wondered if the tub wouldn't give you bruises with all that bouncing," she teased.

Jeff laughed. "After playing football, this was nothing. And I got way more pleasure with you than pounding some guy into the ground."

Allison snuggled closer to him, their bodies still connected. "I don't think I'd want to be on the receiving end of one of your poundings."

His eyes blazed. "Maybe not here. But in a soft bed, you'd feel a whole lot different."

"Yeah?"

"Why don't I step out and clean up while you get the tub going again. We never did get to turn the jets on. Since you wore me out all week and now forced me to bounce in the tub—"

Allison pushed away and took his face in her hands. "Forced you? I can leave right now if you don't want me around."

Jeff dropped his head to kiss first one breast and then the other. "Nah, I like how round some parts of you are." He squeezed her butt. "I also like how soft you are and how good I feel inside you."

With desire once again building up inside her, Allison offered, "How about no bubbles but just jets this time. And more champagne and berries. I don't know about you, but I'm ready for some serious action."

He arched an eyebrow. "This wasn't serious enough for you?"

"Well, maybe for starters. But I'm here for the weekend. I think you'll be very busy showing me a good time."

Jeff moaned as she slid off him and stood. He got up and exited the Jacuzzi. "I do need time to recharge, you know." Offering her his hand, he helped her step onto the tiled floor.

Allison gave him what she hoped was an innocent, angelic look and asked, "Will twenty minutes be enough?"

He moaned again.

They relaxed on the bathroom's padded bench as the tub refilled and drank more champagne and ate berries. When they finished the last berry, she turned toward him, ready for more of his caresses. Her mouth found his, and she relished the urgency of his response. A sharp intake of breath accompanied the squeeze she gave his shaft.

"Recharged yet?"

"Why don't we forget the tub?" Jeff answered with a growl, and he pulled her up. He scooped her into his arms and carried her to the bed.

The night held endless memories for her of their numerous encounters, each better than the last and bringing her to new delightful heights in her quest for fulfillment. She hoped he experienced the same pleasurable satisfaction. Allison loved how protected she felt with his arm wrapped securely around her as he pulled her into his embrace. After many romantic hours, they fell asleep.

When she awoke, she realized Jeff was in a deep sleep, probably trying to make up for lost hours of rest after his long week at the center. Poor guy. He wasn't prepared for the hustle and bustle of caring for kids, but he'd jumped right in and did his part.

She slipped out of his embrace and tiptoed to the bathroom to grab her things. With a quick chuckle, she picked up her teddie—the one she had never gotten to wear. As she went into her room, she made a mental note to try and put it on before Jeff made love with her that evening. Love. Her heart filled with wanting him in her life forever. Did he feel the same way about her?

Allison stepped into her shower and welcomed the soothing spray of water revitalizing her before their day began. She wondered if he still intended to proceed with the plans he'd mentioned the night before. As tempting as the idea of staying naked all weekend sounded, she didn't think either of them would be able to function on Monday if they did.

She scrubbed shampoo into her scalp and inhaled its rich honey scent misting the shower. The water reminded her of wet bodies, bubbles, and climaxing together in a wonderful explosion of sexual desire and release.

Allison hungered for a chance to have it all again, sans the need for protection. Maybe when she married, she and her husband would try the tub version of making babies. Wave after wave of lust could be enjoyed without worrying. Maybe next time, they could add candlelight to the music for more ambiance. She figured setting a sensual scene could only add to any lovemaking encounter.

Her body tingled as she soaped every inch of her skin. Jeff had explored it all, over and over again, never seeming to tire. She'd done the same to his body, surprising herself with her bold teasing and caresses.

She left the shower and wrapped a towel around her. Padding over to the opened, connecting door, she gazed in. Jeff hadn't budged, and she debated over whether to pounce on him, let him sleep, or yell for him to get up.

The first option would set their libidos going, although her quick shower had already jumpstarted hers. The second would be the kind thing to do. The third would act as a reality check for them both. They did need to eat, and maid service would probably expect to have access to the room, even if just for a short while.

Level-headedness won over. Allison chose option number three. She discarded the towel, put on a fluffy robe, and rolled her wet hair in another towel. After walking through their connecting door and over to the bed, she gave him a slight nudge.

Jeff mumbled but didn't open his eyes or make any type of movement. Allison shook him a little harder. This time, the sleepy man opened one eye.

"Why are you out of bed, woman?"

"We need to get up and dressed. You are going to feed me breakfast, aren't you?"

Jeff opened both eyes and blinked. "How about we order room

service and stay indoors?"

"That's all you planned for today? What about doing the tourist thing? You know, seeing the sights—"

His hand reached out and pushed her robe open by her legs. "You're the site I want to see right now."

Jeff's fingers found her sensitive spot and delighted her with teasing strokes, causing her to lean closer to him. The faster he rubbed, the harder she pressed into his hand. He got to his knees by her, placing his other hand around her back for support while his finger continued to swirl around her swollen flesh.

She closed her eyes and lolled back her head. "More. Oh, more," she whispered.

He obliged, pushing her higher until she shook with fulfillment. Spent, she panted while he watched with desire in his eyes.

A knock at the door and a yell of "maid service" startled them both.

"We're still in here!" Jeff hollered. "Give us thirty minutes, please." He mumbled to Allison, "Guess I forgot to put out the do not disturb sign."

Between shallow breaths, Allison remarked, "You didn't get a turn. Do we have time?" Moving in front of him, she placed heated kisses from his neck down his chest.

Jeff eased her away from him. "Honey, we'll never get out of here if you go any further. I'll remember you owe me one. Don't think I'll forget."

"I better go get ready. I need to dry my hair and make myself presentable."

"Fine. And, Allison? Don't put on underwear. I wanna keep that in mind all day while we're out."

Jeff liked the amazed look on her face at his request. It would be a constant turn-on for him all day knowing that under those jeans she'd talked about wearing the night before nothing else touched her skin. The jiggling of her breasts would also keep him craving her.

"Here's something you can do for picture number three. No shorts for you. I'll be checking later to make sure you abide by my request, or picture number three of CEO Jeffrey Ryan drooling while he sleeps hits the Christmas card list," she challenged.

He untied her robe, teasing her skin as he pulled her close to him. "Is that another promise? You, checking on me?"

In a saucy tone, she teased, "Maybe."

"I just need one taste for the road." He moved his head to her breast and sucked on the nipple, fueling an urgent need for her all over again. But he'd promised her he'd show her the sights so he stepped away. "I want you again and again, but that will have to wait until later. Go get dressed."

She cupped his face in her hands and gave him a delicate kiss before leaving.

Jeff flopped back on the bed, amazed he'd had the energy to move at all. His night with Allison had exceeded his wildest dreams, as she'd transformed into a tigress and matched or sometimes surpassed his level of passion.

With the knowledge that he now had less than fifteen minutes to shower, shave, and dress, he tilted forward, ready to get off the bed. A sharper twinge in his side lasted a few seconds. He'd blamed the food and exhaustion for earlier side pains. Laughing to himself, Jeff wondered if this newer pain was the result of too much sex. Could he possibly be getting too old for all this fun and excitement?

Shit. He'd be strong and ignore it. Worse had happened to him on the football field. Winning all those games never came close to satisfying him as much as a sexy vixen named Allison had done in one glorious night. It was probably just a pulled muscle, nothing more.

Chapter Ten

Eyeing him with concern, Allison asked, "Not hungry this morning?" To quiet her stomach rumblings, she stuffed a piece of a jellied bagel into her mouth.

"Guess not." He gave a leering glance. "Maybe I ate too many strawberries last night. And then there's all that champagne you plied me with."

"Oh, I see. Can't keep up with me? I had just as much bubbly as you did, but I'm starving right now."

"True," Jeff whispered, "but I had all that extra champagne to lick off you when you drizzled it all over your body. Not to mention those two strawberries you placed on your—"

"Shhh." She lowered her eyes to her lap and smoothed her napkin.

"Honey, I hope you're not having any regrets. I sure as hell don't. What we experienced was pure heaven. And I want more."

Allison heard the need in his voice, knowing full-well she desired the same. Never before had she reacted so freely with her favors, more than willing to satisfy a man's passion while demanding fulfillment for hers.

Numerous times during their lovemaking, she'd taken charge, giving gentle but no-nonsense directions for what she wanted and telling him what she intended to do. He'd seemed surprised but a willing participant. And, matched her leading the way to climaxing as often as she did.

Foreplay lasted for hours. The teasing, fondling, and tasting had taken Allison to new levels of joy and a desperate need for final release. But here, now, she didn't want to share any of it with others, including strangers who might overhear.

Eyes aimed squarely at his, she said, "I want more too. And no, I don't have any regrets. I wanted this to happen as much as you did." She added a pleading tone to her voice, "But I'd like to keep this private."

"Private it is. I'll do anything to please you." He wiggled his eyebrows and then positioned his mouth closer to her ear. "Is this private enough? I want you to know I'm doing as commanded for picture number three." He slumped back in his chair and took a sip of his coffee.

Allison's body prickled from the feel of his breath on her ear and the image of him sitting so close wearing nothing under his jeans. Her temperature rose a few degrees. She delayed commenting, not trusting herself not to ask for proof and the chance to check him out under the table. Shoving a piece of bacon into her mouth gave her hand something to do and her head time to formulate a response.

Jeff angled his head back near hers. "By the way, are you following my request? I've got these sexy pictures running through my head just thinking about it."

Allison gulped, now having two images to deal with. Hers of him and speculating on his fascination with her. She wore jeans, experiencing the new sensation of the semi-scratchy material rubbing her rear, front, and between her legs. Some positions made her more aware than others of her panty-less condition. Those made her drool and eager to pounce on him.

Could he visualize her body under the jeans? See where the seam of her crotch hit her body? Would he notice where the back curved and stretched to cover her bottom, creasing where her rear met her legs?

"I did exactly as requested. Gotta give you something to think about as we march through the city on our shopping trip. You did say you'd walk everywhere I wanted to go, right?"

Jeff laughed as they stood. "Assuming I can walk, where do you wanna go first?"

Allison gave a thoughtful sigh. "Why don't we just go out the front door, turn in one direction and go where it takes us? Sorta like new tourists not knowing where we're going but just exploring. I'm easy."

"Fine with me. Lead the way."

Allison enjoyed strolling arm in arm with Jeff outside on a warm, sunny day. They went in a men's clothing store since he mentioned wanting to buy some ties. Jeff picked out three, the kind she imagined fathers everywhere cringed at on Christmas or Father's Day.

She jokingly said, "Why on earth do you want these?"

"I see a creative look looming ahead for me. These two," he picked them up, "were inspired by my week with the rugrats, and this one," he pointed to the remaining tie, "is all about you."

"Oh sure. Blame me and the kids because designers everywhere are screaming in protest at your choices."

"So, which one should I wear now? I'll need one for dinner tonight and one for tomorrow. You pick."

After scrutinizing them carefully, Allison pointed to the blue one that depicted hikers or mountain climbers complete with backpacks and green hills in the background. "This one."

Jeff took the tie from her hand and slipped it under the collar of his pale blue oxford shirt. "Thanks. Why this one?"

"Mr. Ryan, I'd think that would be fairly obvious. They're climbers, right? We're hiking, so it goes with our outing."

He knotted the tie and lifted the end up to stare at it. "Nah. I got it to give to the girls at the center so they could play mountain climbing again. I figured this one would remind them of me."

As he paid for the ties and they left the store, Allison's heart melted. The man constantly proved to be a softie, just as Maggie had told her. Kind, loving, thoughtful with kids. Who wouldn't love him?

Jeff interrupted her train of thought. "I looked for ties with an elevator or Jacuzzi on them but didn't see any. We'll have to keep searching for those."

"Why? So you can have people ask about them and have you tell tales about me? No way."

"Damn. They'd be good conversation starters. How about one with strawberries?"

"How about I put pictures number four, five, and six all on the same Christmas card? And send one to your mother?"

"Here's a deal for you. You stop the blackmail, and I won't get more ties." He lifted her chin and placed a delicate kiss on her lips. "Although, you can go ahead and send those pictures to my mother. She adores kids, and someday I want her to have grandchildren."

"Randy Ryan wants children?" Allison teased.

"Honey, you can call me that anytime you want, but only if it's in connection to you." Jeff's stare penetrated her soul. "I do want a family someday."

She smiled, not knowing where the conversation should go from there. Having him randy only for her would please her to no end, and to hell with the gossips and their stories. Tales would no doubt travel like wildfire throughout the company once word of their affair surfaced.

This weekend was for them and not for any "I won, you lost" dare. Right? Too many questions began crowding her head, offering a potential unhappy outcome. For now, they were happy, and that was the only thing she wanted to concentrate on.

Jeff took her hand and tucked it under his arm. "How about if we go back now. I need to rest. For some strange reason, I didn't get enough sleep this past week, and then last night someone kept me awake."

"I know what you mean," Allison offered with an exaggerated yawn. "Same thing happened to me. Well, just last night's part."

With a sparkle in his eyes, he asked, "Miss Allison, what's it to be? My place or yours?"

"I'll think about it as we walk back."

The short distance to the hotel didn't take too long. They strolled along a street lined with tourist shops filled with everything from designer clothes to antiques. Once inside the hotel and outside their suite doors, Allison made her decision.

"I need to freshen up a little. I'll leave the connecting door open. Why don't you come over in about fifteen minutes?"

"We have a few hours before dinner. Think we can find something to fill up the time?" Jeff reached for her face, stroking a finger down her nose to her mouth. She puckered her lips and kissed it.

"I'll come up with something." Allison swiveled her hips and strolled into her room in an attempt to provoke him. Hearing his groan, she knew she'd succeeded.

Twenty minutes later, she realized no sounds came from his room. Allison had already taken a quick shower and slipped into her pink negligee. She peered through the door, only to find Jeff sprawled out and sleeping on one of the sofas. He'd removed his shirt and tie, but his jeans remained on his body. He lay flat on his stomach with one arm and one leg dangling over the edge. Tiny snoring sounds broke through the silence of the room.

Allison noted the slow, even rise and fall of his back as he slept. She decided not to wake him and padded into his bathroom to get his robe. Back at his side, she gently placed it on him.

Jeff stirred, still half-asleep. "I'll get up in a minute. How about a quick massage? Would you mind?"

"Not at all. You rest. I'll take care of you," she whispered.

Lifting the robe off him, Allison shifted closer to reach his shoulders. First, though, she tucked his leg onto the couch as he pulled his dangling arm closer to his body. She noticed that his jeans had slid down a little on his body and figured he'd unzipped them to make himself more comfortable.

The touch of her hands on his shoulders sent flashes of heat soaring through her. She kneaded his muscles with circular, probing motions, hearing his soft sighs fade into the even breathing of sleep. She lowered her hands down his back and trailed her nails along his skin, more for her benefit than his. Down, down, down they continued and stopped at the edge of his jeans.

Allison ran the fingertips of one hand along the inside of his waist band area. Jeff hadn't worn shorts, and the itch to move her hand as far as the material would stretch caused blood to pump faster in her veins. Damn. Like a horny teenager experiencing the early wonders of sex and the power of being in control, Allison yearned to let her hand stray.

As much as she wanted him, he was exhausted. She had to let him rest. They had the whole night and next day to enjoy each other's body again and again. Taking advantage of him, or just waking him up to do so, wouldn't show control. With every shred of willpower she possessed, she pulled her hand back, grabbed his robe, and placed it over him.

Allison sighed and softly tiptoed back to her room, resisting the urge to prance out the door like an alley cat on the prowl. She changed and watched TV for a couple of hours before he softly knocked on the door.

"I'm embarrassed about falling asleep and leaving you alone. Sorry." Sincerity edged Jeff's tone. "Should we get some dinner?"

"Sure." Deciding not to dwell on his napping, Allison grabbed her purse and walked out the door with him.

He tucked her hand in the crook of his arm as they waited for the elevator. She noticed him wince slightly as he shifted his body during their ride to the hotel's restaurant floor. After being greeted by the hostess, they were seated at a table overlooking the street.

"I'm sorry. That's really never happened to me before." Jeff frowned. "Falling asleep and leaving a beautiful woman waiting inches away isn't very friendly." He offered his apology for the third time since they'd left their suites.

"Hmm. Now I'm curious about all the gossiped tales of your escapades. I'm starting to feel like just one in a crowd of your admirers." Allison raised her wine glass and took a sip.

"Don't believe the stories. You're special to me. Please believe that."

"You're special to me, too." She placed a hand on his arm. "Jeff, I wonder if news of our relationship will lead to more stories flying throughout your company. What will people think?"

He winked and covered her hand with his. "That I'm a lucky man to have you?"

"You know what I mean. If you do agree to my request, will the gossips think I slept with you to get what I wanted?"

In a serious tone, he answered, "My personal life is nobody's business. If I agree to funding for the center, the only one whose opinion I'd care about is yours. And I hope you don't think I'd barter what we had for material things."

Knots formed in the pit of her stomach as she processed his choice of words. Had, not have? As in maybe it's over or will be soon? "I'd never use my body for—"

"Honey," he drawled, "you use it really well from my standpoint."

"I wouldn't use sex for bargaining purposes. But the center needs financial help." Tension flooded her system.

Jeff blinked, trying hard to figure out what was going on in that pretty little female mind of hers. Their time together had been pure magic. She said she didn't bargain with her body. Didn't want it used. Then she threw in her comment about the center needing money. Uneasiness between them loomed ahead if they didn't talk about something else.

"So, how do you like this tie?" He steered them back to the cozy and comfortable conversation they'd enjoyed before.

Allison smiled and tilted back in her seat as her eyes drifted down from his face to his tie. "Hmm. Black background with smiling faces on it. Many different colors of faces."

"Yep. And it reminds you of?"

"What a happy man you are?" She grinned and then took another drink of wine from her glass.

Jeff waved his finger at her. "No, no, no. Think harder. Tuesday.

Field trip. Rose bush. You drooling over my smiley underwear."

"Me? Do you have pictures of me drooling?"

"No, but I saw it in living color."

"And I have another picture I just remembered to add to my collection for that Christmas card. Or, maybe I should plan a calendar."

Jeff drained his glass and stared at her through narrowed eyes. "Didn't I already bargain for those six pictures? You can't use them."

"Maybe not, but I confess. I took more than six. And, then there's Susan's masterpiece. It's still hanging on the kitchen wall, right next to the refrigerator."

He leaned in closer to her and uttered in a husky voice, "I'm not wearing those smiley shorts tonight. I'm actually not wearing any at all. Are you naked under that dress?"

A red stain crept up Allison's cheeks. Jeff surmised that only the satiny fabric separated his hands from her body.

"I'm doing what you asked." She took a deep breath, and he moaned as her dress clung tighter around her breasts. "You're trying to distract me from my blackmailing. I really do have more pictures. Took some when you slept with Dawn. Then snuck in a few others when you weren't looking."

He laughed. "You are one devious woman. So you think you'll make a calendar using pictures of me? Wouldn't you rather have me pose for you? I could get in that Jacuzzi and give you some great shots."

"Oh, I'm not sure about the posing part. The candid shots always interest people more. Unless we do a hunk-type of calendar. You know, we'd probably make more money that way."

"Did you say 'we'? So I'll get paid?" Jeff asked with a wink.

Allison's hand landed on his knee. His body jolted in reaction to her intimate touch as her fingertips traced lines up and down his thigh and brushed his crotch.

"Sure I'll pay you. Models get paid. We could call it Ryan's Rugrats: Hunky CEO. Hmm." She looked deep in thought.

"Could be a great fundraiser for the center. And the title kinda grabs attention."

His arousal grew with every stroke she brushed against his zippered area. She ran a fingernail down the length of his manhood, causing it to twitch. Jeff's breathing sped, and he captured her hand, stilling her actions.

Almost panting, he managed to say, "We'd have to discuss my salary. I'm not cheap, but you may be able to convince me to pose for free. I'll have to think about it. Since we're done here, why don't we go into the lounge area to dance?"

Mischief sparkled in her eyes. "I'm ready. For anything. But dancing's a good place to start."

After Jeff paid for their meal, he escorted her from the lush dining room setting and out into the colorfully decorated hallway. The sounds of casual dance music floated through the air as they neared the Romantic Rendezvous Lounge. Without giving her a chance to sit, he walked with her onto the wood-paneled dance floor and folded her into his embrace.

Jeff's hand rested comfortably on the small of her back, his finger gently stroking the area. He couldn't help but notice how well their bodies fit together as he held her tightly to him. Her ability to change steps to suit each number made dancing with Allison more pleasurable.

No more talk was made about the center or using bodies. She didn't bring up the subjects again, and he definitely wouldn't revisit those issues either. At least not right now. Spending their remaining weekend time together in complete and utter harmony suited his desires.

"I love dancing with you. You fit great in my arms." Jeff snuggled her closer within his grip.

The friction caused by her breasts rubbing through the material of her dress against his shirt caused erotic fantasies to flood his brain. He inhaled her familiar honey and rose scent and longed to make love to her again.

"Umm. I could do this for hours. Did the professor's wife teach you to dance?"

"No. She was too busy teaching me things I could do lying down, not standing up. I learned this at boarding school. Even at a military school, you have to know the proper social graces to move up the ranks."

"And did you?"

He tensed for a second before answering, and then released her hand to rub his side. With a half-smile, he remarked, "Let's sit this one out. Guess I pulled a muscle sometime this week, and all this dancing jolted it again."

With a look of concern on her face, Allison stated, "Of course. I'm sorry if I made you go crazy with the kids and everything. I didn't mean to wreak havoc on your body."

They sat at a table for two and ordered drinks. Soft music and dimmed lights set a romantic mood around them.

"I'm fine. The kids did keep me active, but for that matter, so did you. One-on-one with you is a much better and more interesting exercise."

"I'll take that as a compliment." Allison reached for her glass and sipped. "Umm, This Singapore Sling is great."

"Watch out for the kicker in those. That fruit starts out easy, but then the liquor gets you when you least expect it. I bartended my way through college. Well, sorta on the side since I was underage most of the time." Jeff took a gulp of his brandy.

After clearing her throat, she summarized aloud, "So Randy Ryan got to serve drinks and chase the girls. Sounds like you partied your way through school."

"Hey, I also took ROTC." He shrugged. "I've always been a flag-waver."

While slouching back in her chair, Allison said, "I enjoy all the tidbits of information about your life that you toss out. An affair with a professor's wife. Illegal bartending. Joined ROTC because you're patriotic."

"Good thing you're not a reporter. I guess I'm just really comfortable talking to you."

Allison crossed her heart with her hand. "Not a reporter. Just curious. What branch of the military were you in?"

"Four years in the Army. I debated whether or not to stay in and make it a career or enter the family business." A knot of sadness twisted in his stomach. "But when my father died, I made the right choice and stayed here."

"We have something in common, sort of. I'm an ex-military brat. Moved everywhere, thanks to the Army. Dad did love his career."

"I guess he's retired now."

In a soft, heartrending tone, she replied, "He never got the chance. My parents died in a car crash five years ago."

Commiserating with her, Jeff squeezed her hand and leaned over to plant a quick kiss on her forehead. "Sorry to hear that, honey. Were you living here?"

"No. I was teaching in Virginia, but I decided to move near my Aunt Abigail. She's the only family I have left."

"Now I've learned something about you I didn't know. A teacher, huh? I thought you worked for some computer company before Ryan's Rugrats."

"I did. But teaching's always been my passion. The computer company had me working on educational stuff for schools, but I missed being with the kids."

"My sister's a nun and teaches second grade. Sister Margaret Mary is my mother's joy. I'm her cross to bear. You've already heard all her tales of woe about me."

Jeff marveled at how easy it had been to share facets of their lives with each other. Some parts meshed with each other's like teaching, the military, dancing, and without a doubt, strong sexual appetites.

From what Allison had mentioned about Michael, he'd appeared as selfish as Laura. A wham-bam-thank-you-ma'am kind of guy, Michael had shown no interest in Allison's needs and made her hesitant to ask for what she wanted. Jeff soured on the thought of someone hurting her.

He hoped she viewed him differently than Michael as his main desire was to make her happy. He didn't care if she climaxed more times than he did. It also didn't matter if he couldn't recharge as quickly as she apparently could. And that had surprised both of them.

"How about driving to a great secluded place I know where we can view the city?" Jeff suggested, after wondering if he'd be able to come up with something to surprise Allison.

"Got all your favorite spots mapped out, huh? Do you take all your dates where we're going?"

"Nah." He swallowed the remainder of his drink. "Actually, I haven't done this since the summer after I graduated from high school. Hot-to-trot Heather was most obliging with her favors. Unfortunately, I found out she did that on a regular basis with more than just me. She left me crushed and heartsick when I found out."

Allison drained her glass. "I'm ready to go if you are."

"We'll get my car for this. I don't think I want a cab driver finding my secret spot and turning it into a tourist attraction."

They got up from their lounge table, and she slid her arm around his waist. He wrapped his arm around her shoulders and led her out of the lounge and down to the lobby. While waiting for his car to be brought around to the front, Jeff noticed a man giving Allison a thorough once-over. Upset at this man's intrusion into their cozy couple status, a protective and jealous instinct kick in. He wanted Allison all to himself for lots of reasons that paraded through his brain…some he was just beginning to understand.

He helped her into his car, got in, and drove toward Berkley Park, their destination for the evening. She rested her hand on his thigh and gave a gentle squeeze, arousing his desire to make love to her.

Comfortable around her and with a desire to have her stay by his side, Jeff couldn't stop a smile from forming. After their hectic but short, enticing week together, he realized that the words love and Allison sounded great together in one sentence. And, more importantly, he didn't mind the connection at all.

Chapter Eleven

Allison loved the city view at night. "It's so beautiful out here. Real quiet and peaceful," she commented as Jeff parked the car overlooking the Kansas City skyline.

"I guess we're not the only ones who think that." He pointed to a white Ford truck parked to their left. "I wonder what they're doing in there to make it shake like an earthquake's centered under it."

"Probably something like this." She ran her hand up his thigh and pressed it into his crotch, rubbing her palm over the already bulging area.

"Lord, honey, you don't give a guy a minute to relax. Good thing I'm all rested up."

Jeff slipped his arm around her shoulders and hugged her to him. He angled his head to reach her lips and traced his tongue along each one. As she continued massaging his zippered area, a catch in his breathing turned into a moan of desire.

At first, his kiss entailed lips-on-lips only. When she opened her mouth, his tongue darted inside. Allison closed down slightly, giving him a narrow area to dart his tongue in and out of, mimicking the ultimate consummating act of love.

When his hand reached out to fondle her breast, a wickedly naughty thought popped into her head. She pulled back and asked with a purr, "Just what kind of shape are you in?"

Jeff whooshed out one long exhale, and a glazed look accompanied his response. "Like I've been telling you, anything you can do, I can do."

Her hand returned to his zipper, and she eased it down in minute movements. "Can you do this?" She skimmed one fingernail along his skin under the unzipped area.

Clearing his throat, Jeff replied, "That's something I only want you to do. Am I in the right shape for you now?"

"Hmm, actually this shape is fine. But that's not what I meant."

Jeff grabbed her hand, pressing her palm on him. The slacks front pulled open, and she relished the bulky feel of his arousal in her grasp.

"Tell me now before I go insane from lack of oxygen."

"You'll do what I say?" Dictating orders gave Allison an unashamed sense of her own sensuality and control.

"Tell me."

"Get in the backseat."

Heavy breathing filled the air between them. Without another word, he pushed away, opened his car door while holding his pants with one hand, and exited the car. He peered at her through the driver's side window.

"Are you joining me? I don't wanna play by myself. You're much more interesting and friendly."

"Oh? And what about Hot-to-trot Heather? Did she play nice in the backseat with you?" Allison smiled and fluttered her eyelashes.

"Sometimes. Then again, rumor had it she was very familiar with backseats," Jeff said. "Something tells me you can show me things Heather never thought of. You're much older than she was when I knew her."

Allison ran her tongue along her lips in a sensual, teasing motion. "Old, huh? How about adventurous? Creative?"

"Woman, the backseat's waiting for us. Besides, horny, passionate, or sexy would be better adjectives for you." A lusty tone entered his voice. "I want you now."

She got out, and they slid into the backseat. To rouse his curiosity, Allison quipped, "To show you how creative I am, let's try something different."

Jeff eyed her with a sly grin on his face. "Haven't we been doing that every time we get naked?"

She gave him her best I'm-the-teacher look and explained, "We'll each take off one piece of clothing at the same time and only touch when the clothing's gone."

He laughed. "How long does this go on? I can only control myself so far."

"How about if I add tasting to the list of what we can do?"

Raw desire flamed in his eyes, and he let out a deep, ragged sigh. "Let's start. What comes off first?"

"Your shirt and tie. Unzip my dress so I can push the top down to my waist."

Jeff removed his things. He reached behind her and quickly did as asked. Moonlight reflected off Jeff's chest, and Allison longed to run her hands along his skin and tweak his nipples until they hardened. He wasted no time in reaching over to her breasts. He rolled her nipples between his thumbs and forefingers until the tips beaded into hardened peaks.

She ached for more caresses. Her hands ran up his chest and pinched each nipple. Jeff gave a quick inhale at her touch. He lifted a breast and lowered his head. Allison's heartbeat raced in wanton anticipation. As he licked and sucked on her nipple, Allison's hand strayed down his chest to his pants. Her fingers caressed his shaft, and Jeff moaned at her intimate massage.

A noise outside their car stilled their actions, and they wrenched away from each other.

"Is someone out there?" Jeff looked back and forth through the windows.

Allison, panting and heated with need, checked the outside while covering her breasts with her hands. "I don't see anyone."

Jeff sank back against the seat. "Whew. We sure forget our surroundings when you keep me busy."

She gave him a slight nudge. "You mean when we keep each other busy."

"Anything you say. It all boils down to the fact that I lose my mind around you."

Allison dropped her arms to her waist and rested back on the seat. "Maybe we should head to the hotel for more privacy. Getting caught by the police wouldn't look good for either of us."

"Yep, I know what you mean. We're not teenagers anymore. Just horny adults. Sure heightens the excitement, though."

"Save that thought for later," she offered as she slipped back into the top of her dress and turned her back to him.

He zipped her dress. "You still haven't drowned me. Guess I'm on your good list," he offered and grabbed his shirt and tie. "Although, you still have all night and tomorrow."

"Thanks for reminding me." She leaned toward him and feathered a light kiss on his lips. "I'll keep that in mind," she teased.

After they'd pulled their clothes into some semblance of order, they returned to the front seat. As Jeff drove back to the hotel, Allison wondered at his choice of words. While happy knowing more lovemaking would soon follow, he'd said "All night and tomorrow." Would there be anything for them as a couple after that?

"You're awfully quiet. Tired?"

"No. Just trying to get my head together. I seem to lose my inhibitions around you," she joked.

"I like you that way, Miss Alley Cat." He shrugged. "Just save your explorations for me."

"Now how can I promise that? I'm an alley cat, remember? Nobody ties us down."

"Well I can only try. You know, another idea just occurred to me. We could use my ties and—"

"No way. I want my hands and yours free to roam. Maybe some other time." Would there be another time after their weekend ended?

"No ties, huh? Will you still want me without the champagne and strawberries?" Jeff's fingers gripped the steering wheel.

Allison had a desperate need to have his fingers caress her instead. "I'll take you with or without the extras."

"No boyfriends waiting in the wings?"

Michael had made enough promises to her that she'd thought they'd have a life together. When he'd left, she had avoided dates to give her heart a safe refuge from heartache. Until now. Was her heart safe with Jeff?

"I've only had one real relationship, the one I mentioned earlier. Guess I'm not as experienced as you are."

"Allison, where did you learn all that we've been doing?" Jeff gave a hearty laugh. "Got a secret life as a voyeur? Or do you watch X-rated movies?"

"Nope. I read lots of romance books. All kinds, from sweet to erotic."

"Man. I've been reading the wrong stuff. If you picked up all those tips from romance books, I may need to read some to keep up with you. Hell, you could surpass me, lose interest, and then where would I be?"

Allison caressed the back of his neck and then placed her hand on his groin. A low groan escaped from his lips. She kneaded him through the material of his slacks. "I haven't lost interest yet. And, I'd say you haven't either."

Jeff slowed their speed as he maneuvered the car into a line of vehicles waiting for the valet parking attendant. "Keep in mind we have to walk through the lobby. Don't get me stirred up until after we get upstairs."

She gave one more rub and then removed her hand.

They exited the car, walked through the plush hotel lobby, and entered the empty elevator for a quick ride up to their rooms. After taking her swiftly into his embrace, Jeff gave Allison a passionate kiss. He pulled his head back, and she rested her head on his chest.

In a teasing tone, she mentioned, "I've enjoyed you staring at me today, knowing I was braless."

Jeff squeezed her more tightly into his embrace. "Not a second went by that I didn't think about it. Stay that way."

"Whatever you say." She pulled out of his arms as the elevator door opened. "It's your turn to be in charge."

"Damn right."

They walked to their doors, and Allison glanced at him while desire coursed through her veins. "Where are we tonight?"

"Your place. I'll be over in fifteen minutes. I'm ordering more dessert for us. What would you like?"

Licking her lips, Allison remembered one decadent treat she'd spied on the menu. "Chocolate mousse. I adore that stuff. And a small brandy."

"What should I order?" He tipped his head in thought. "I'll surprise you. You'll share with me, won't you? I intend to share mine with you."

"Sharing's good. Just pick something different. Come into my room when you have everything. I'm gonna take a quick shower."

Jeff pointed a finger at her and drawled, "No. We'll do that together later."

Allison entered her room and inhaled a deep breath. Another night of desires and fantasy lie ahead, and she tingled with a lusty eagerness to have him to herself.

She changed into her negligee and robe, the one she'd bought Thursday night, fully expecting to be Jeff's guest for the weekend. She loved the feel of the nylon, still new and somewhat scratchy on her skin. Practically see-through, she decided to don a skimpy pink lace thong to add to her allure. Like he needed any more encouragement.

Her normal nighttime attire consisted of cotton pajamas, not anything to entice a lover into a frenzy of sexual arousal, but it was definitely practical for sleeping alone. And she'd done enough of that most of her life.

Sleeping with Michael had been an educational exercise of male satisfaction and female frustration. He'd bought her a cotton nightgown with buttons down the front and explained that it was more practical for her to unbutton the front. He'd enter her, caress her breasts, and all too soon their lovemaking would be over.

Allison would then lay awake, wondering what was wrong with her. Obviously he didn't find her attractive enough to want her in anything pretty or sexy. She was handy, a body to use for his release while she never got the same satisfaction.

Jeff worshiped her body, as she did his. She raised her head up to the heavens "And," she said aloud, "I love him."

A knock on the connecting door startled her for a second. She smiled to herself and yelled, "Who is it?"

The voice on the other side of the door answered, "A stranger bearing gifts. Are you busy tonight?"

Allison ambled over and opened the door, blocking his entrance as she pretended to check him out to decide if she would let him in. "I've gotta see what you brought first. I just can't let in any stranger trying to bribe his way into my good graces."

Falling into his role, Jeff replied smoothly, "It's not your good graces I want into. But see," he pointed to her chocolate mousse on a dessert cart, "I think I have something here you really want."

"Ah. A stranger with mousse. Is that all you have?" She rubbed her hands over her body. His eyes widened, and Allison untied the robe's bow, allowing the flimsy material to slip from her body.

"Pretty color. Can I interest you in a brandy?"

She watched the rise and fall of his chest as it pressed against the silky fabric of his robe. Allison couldn't miss the growing bulge below his tied belt.

"Yes, thank you. Is that all? No surprise dessert? I see something else I want," she took a quick glance at his groin. "Did you bring anything else to entice me?"

"How about this?" Jeff uncovered a plate holding a piece

of strawberry shortcake, complete with berries and globs of whipped cream.

Donning a nonchalant guise, Allison muttered, "I had berries yesterday. Not very original."

"True, but you don't know what I'm going to do with the whipped cream, now do you?" He wiggled his eyebrows and put a dab on her nose.

Allison looked cross-eyed at the white fluff. "Can't say that does anything for me."

Jeff pushed the door open, leaned near her, and licked the cream off. "That was just to get me through the door. I have lots of other places I plan to put this stuff. All I need is a willing model. Preferably someone who's not ticklish but likes to squirm."

"You found your model." Allison stepped to the side so Jeff could wheel in the cart. "But that means you get to model too."

Once again, the night seemed to progress with one erotic encounter after another. Jeff fulfilled all her desires, and she reveled in total sexual satisfaction. Pleasing him had become her goal, and Allison delighted in participating in any requests he made. When they finally settled into bed to sleep while curled together, she knew her dreams would be pleasant and peaceful.

Mid-morning, Allison awoke first, her back to Jeff and enveloped in his arms. Sunday. The last day of their weekend. She snuggled in closer to him.

"Hey, sleepyhead. We need to get up. We have places to go and things to do before the night's over." His voice sounded gravelly as he spoke into her ear.

"What's on for today?"

Jeff eased his arms from around her body, and Allison noticed the sudden absence of the protective heat that had encased her.

"I don't know about you, but I'm starving. Let's get breakfast, and then we'll check out. We'll drive to your place, so you can drop off your car. Then, it's off to see the Royals trounce the Yankees. Hope you like baseball."

Allison smiled and watched as he put on his robe. She would love waking up with him on Sundays, lounging around for a lazy day of rest and fun. Actually, any day would be just as pleasant if they were together.

"I adore baseball." She eased herself out of bed, stretched while she yawned, and then swayed her hips as she walked to the bathroom. Before disappearing and closing the door, she added, "I'll be ready in twenty minutes. Is that okay?"

"Whenever you're ready, meet me in my room."

Half an hour later, Allison enjoyed their casual chatting throughout breakfast. She welcomed his additional stories of childhood memories, college classes, and work. These glimpses into Jeff's past and present life made him more of a comfortable presence who could easily fit into her life. He'd appeared just as eager at listening to her stories, and she warmed at his rapt attention and eagerness at laughing along with her at her funny stories. Opening up to him and letting Jeff into her heart came natural.

Allison's first break from Jeff's continuous company since Friday came as she drove her car to her apartment. It felt odd not having him so close, and an anxious emptiness filled the pit of her stomach. Would this be it? Would their weekend end and all they'd shared become just memories of someone she had once loved who walked out of her life?

Easing the tension and determined to concentrate on happier thoughts, she parked her car and waited for him to pull into her parking lot. Allison leaned against the hood, waving at him as he drove up.

"Hey, lady. I've got two tickets to the ball game. Wanna go?" he yelled from his window.

"Interesting pick-up line," she teased.

"Works all the time. I get all my dates this way. I just cruise around looking for sexy women." He waved tickets by the window and gave her a devilish grin. "Feeling lucky?"

"I guess you'll do. It's you who's lucky."

Allison waltzed to his car and got in. He gave her a wink that curled her toes and made her pulse race. She wanted the feeling to last a lifetime.

On the way to the stadium, Jeff relaxed at her witty responses to his joking comments. "I hope you're not one of those closeted Yankee fans. You will root for the Royals, won't you?

"Go Royals." She fidgeted in her seat. "So, are you going to buy me hot dogs and peanuts?"

He took a quick peek at her and loved the glowing look on her face. "Sure. Gotta keep you happy."

Denying he'd fallen in love with her would be a lost cause. Where would their relationship go after the weekend? He sure as hell wanted it to continue and prayed she did too. They definitely enjoyed incredible sexual satisfaction, and all indications pointed to compatible likes and dislikes. But it took more than that to make a lifetime commitment work for two people. Loyalty, honesty, and devotion, just to name a few.

Laura never knew the meaning of those words. From what Allison had told him, neither had Michael. He and Allison had both been betrayed and used by people they loved. Trusting her would involve an enormous amount of faith and love, leaving his heart vulnerable.

"I've never been this close to the dugout before. I'll be able to see the guys clearly from here," Allison said as Jeff led her to their seats.

"This is a company box. We give away half of our season tickets to employees."

"Nice gesture." She gave him a shy smile, and he handed her a program. "Thanks. I'll show it to Aunt Abigail. She's a real fan. Even yells at the umpires."

"Sounds like she and my mother would hit it off. Hell, throw in Maggie and that'd be a threesome to avoid, because you'd never win an argument."

Flipping through the pages of her program, Allison asked, "And what about me?"

"You," he answered as he ran his finger along her cheek and down to her chin, "don't yell except when I goofed up at the center."

Allison let out a laugh. "You forgot their painting aprons and made a mess on the carpet. Of course, your pants took the brunt of Susan's spilled paint jars."

"You run a pretty tight ship and things probably go more smoothly when I'm not around to add confusion to the controlled chaos." He leaned in to whisper, "And your level of experience goes without saying."

The air crackled with sparks of electricity dancing between them, even out in the open and surrounded by thousands of cheering fans. Allison only heard his voice and the seductive implication in his choice of words.

Experience? Her? Most everything they'd done registered as a new adventure. Maybe she'd been so repressed and horny that her natural sexual instincts had taken over, guiding her to do, say, and try things she never imagined she'd be capable of. With Jeff it had all come so easy.

Those romance books had also come in handy. Besides fantasizing about handsome lovers all those long, quiet nights she'd spent alone, some of the actions and seductive scenes somehow had planted seeds of knowledge in her brain. Those images of carnal knowledge had germinated, just waiting for the right man to come along. She'd just harvested her crop of ideas and acted on them.

Maybe the chapter in her life's book detailing her sexual awakening needed to be expanded to two chapters. Or even more when she considered all the wonderful, and sometimes decadent, ways they'd pleased each other. In fact, the last thing they'd tried before sleeping last night involved fully opening their drapes so moonlight shone in, highlighting their bodies as they—

"So, how many do you want?"

Jeff's interruption distracted her. "Huh?"

"Honey, quit daydreaming. How many hotdogs do you want?

What kind of drink? Want peanuts too?"

That brought a smile to her face. "Two hotdogs with relish, mustard, and sauerkraut. Iced tea and lots of peanuts."

"Stay put and don't talk to strangers." He winked and said in a hushed tone, "I know how easy it is to have my way with you if the right food's offered. I don't want any stranger barging in. Lucky for me there's no chocolate mousse in the ballpark."

Allison purposely licked her lips, doing it slowly as she noticed his eyes follow her tongue's path. "And suppose that's what I craved right now?"

Jeff grinned and leaned closer to give her a quick kiss. "Save that thought for later. If you want mousse, I'll get you some after we have dinner. We'll need something to top our weekend off, and that sure appeals to me."

So far, he'd mentioned the game, dinner, and now a hint of one last lovemaking session. Cinderella would turn back into a nine-to-five working girl tomorrow, and the prince would hop on a plane for a business trip. Would the prince turn into a toad, leaving her nothing more than another statistic to add to Randy Ryan's list of conquests?

The time at the ballpark went all too quickly to suit Allison's taste. She savored every moment they'd spent together, even at the game, and thought about his smiles, laughter, and the tangy scent of his cologne.

Jeff hugged Allison to his side as they walked back to his car. "It's always good to win, but to beat the Yankees makes it special."

"I know what you mean. Winning is great," she agreed.

"Hmm. Glad to hear you say that."

"Why?"

"Because I won your challenge and survived a week with the rugrats."

A shiver careened down her spine. Was this his way of telling her what they'd shared boiled down to nothing more than just his prize as the winner?

"Is winning so important to you?" she queried in a somber tone.

"Sometimes it's the only thing that counts. Other times, it's all about how you get there and the results." He kissed her head. "You're a great consequence."

Allison yanked away from him, ready to unleash her hurt feelings. She prepared to initiate a royal battle with the now almost-toad standing beside her.

"I'm not some winner's prize. Do you think I stayed with you only because you won?" Her voice elevated a few levels as she aimed her comment at him.

He unlocked his car and stared at her with a blank look masking his face. "What are you talking about? Of course I don't think that. Where did that come from?"

"Maybe this weekend's over now." She shook her head. "You don't really care about me or the center, do you?"

Chapter Twelve

Jeff couldn't help an uneasy feeling creeping into his body. Was this her entrance to a fight, placing the center and her demands up front?

"Let's just get in the car and discuss this over dinner. I think we're getting too confused over what's going on." He softened his voice. "Please, get in."

Tears made her eyes sparkle, and he wanted nothing more than to crush her in his arms and agree to anything she wanted to stop their flow. But this had to be resolved. She hesitated, and he wondered if she'd walk away from him right there in the stadium's parking lot. If she did, she'd be out of his life.

And that would break his heart.

"You're right. We need to talk." Her voice sounded shaky, and she continued blinking back tears.

Unfortunately, Laura had pulled the same ploy on him many times. Too many to count. Tears eventually didn't work on him from Laura, but Allison was different. He wanted it to be different with her.

"You choose a place for dinner. Anywhere's fine with me. Maybe someplace closer to your apartment," Jeff remarked in an almost business-like manner.

With just a nod, Allison got in his car. Jeff started the engine and turned on the radio. Some soothing music appealed to him, and he hoped it would give her a chance to regain her composure.

As he entered the highway, he asked, "Have you thought of a place for dinner?"

"The Bristol isn't too far from my apartment."

"Good choice. I like their food." After taking in a deep breath, he pleaded, "Please, let's not talk about anything right now except pleasant things."

"Actually, we don't have to talk as you drive. The music's great, and this is my favorite station."

He detected sadness in her voice but tried to concentrate on driving. Every time he peeked at her, Allison's head was turned toward the window. Occasionally he'd hear her softly singing along with the music, but other than that, they didn't speak.

As they drove, Allison tried to puzzle things out. What did she want from him? Respect, honesty, trust, love. All of those things topped her list. Was it too soon for love? Maybe, but that could come if the other things were there.

What would she accept? Those same first three things would be vital. If he didn't love her and just wanted an affair, maybe she could handle that. Lots of romances never got around to love but seemed to flourish. She could love him, she did love him, and that could be enough for them both.

She couldn't stop a sad smile from curving her mouth. Who was she trying to fool? She wanted it all—to love a man unconditionally and have his love in return. It would break her heart if Jeff didn't love her. He could leave her after their weekend or stay and not love her.

Damn. My heart will break either way.

Their ride seemed endless until they finally reached the restaurant and walked inside. After ordering, Jeff took her hand in his and made eye contact, something they'd avoided since leaving the stadium.

"Allison, I've loved every moment I've spent with you and not because I won that silly challenge. You made our time together special. I don't know how else to say it. I guess I don't know what you expect from me."

His plea softened her heart. "I'm confused about our relationship. Is it over between us after tonight?"

His surprised look caught her off-guard. "Of course not. Look," he took a deep breath and let it out slowly, "can't we just have the rest of the night as two people crazy about each other?"

Some of the nervous jitters parading in her stomach relaxed, although niggling doubts and questions remained.

"And tomorrow? What happens then?" She had to know, to prepare her heart.

"Tomorrow," he answered, "I go to St. Louis, and you go to work. I'll call you from there, and we'll talk. I may have to stay there longer than a day, so I can't make any definite plans right now."

Allison turned her hand in his and squeezed, content with the warmth it gave her. Smiling at him she responded, "I'll wait for your call."

She fell comfortably into relaxing during their leisurely dinner. Allison noted that Jeff made the same effort she did at keeping their conversation centered on mundane subjects minus any sexual innuendoes.

The casual ease of their weekend returned, and Allison loved his caring questions and attention. All too soon, the time had flown by, and they arrived at her apartment. She prayed it wouldn't be her last chance to be held in his arms while they enjoyed each other's passion.

Their rush to make love started by her door as she fumbled with her keys. Jeff ran his hand up and down her bottom. Once inside, a flurry of clothes hit the floor in record time as they undressed. His lust-filled eyes glued onto hers.

"Leave that tie on," she demanded.

Jeff gave a lazy grin. "You like champagne glasses on ties, huh? I guess my third choice also holds a special meaning for you."

"I want to remember what we did in that Jacuzzi while we

make love."

"Where's the bedroom?" His question came out as an urgent demand.

"No. Not there. I want to try something different." Allison gave him what she hoped was a saucy look and wiggled a finger at him. "This way, Randy."

He growled. "Oh, I see, Miss Alley Cat. Your place, you're in control again. I guess I better go quietly." He gave a devilish smirk. "Unless you want me to be noisy for the neighbors."

While leading the way over to her oversized recliner, she said, "I hear them all the time. Maybe it's time they heard me." Allison threw a quilt on the leather chair, patted it down, and bent over to give Jeff a full, unavoidable view of her rear.

Blowing out a ragged breath, he moved over to her, grabbed her from behind and ground on her bottom. His hands went around to her breasts, and he caressed each one, making the nipples bead in his fingers.

Allison tilted her head back and closed her eyes. Oh, yes, this was what she wanted. She hoped it wouldn't be a final performance for the two of them. She pulled away and took hold of his tie. Reeling him in near her, she ordered him to sit in the recliner. Once he was settled there, she knelt before him, never breaking eye contact. Very slowly, she inched her hands up his thighs to rest on the curly-haired bulge between his legs.

Warm hands met hot turgid flesh that begged for her attention. She then eased open his knees and placed her lips where her hands had been. Jeff's moan stirred her on to swifter and more urgent caresses. Her tongue glided up and down on his shaft, licking and teasing as it moved.

"Honey," he said in an almost breathless voice, "I can't take much more of that. I'd love nothing more than to finish right here."

Allison gave him one small nip before moving, relishing the way he held his breath before panting again.

"Hmm. I'd say you're ready for me," she teased.

"Absolutely. But first, take a condom out of my pocket. The right one."

On shaky legs and ripe with need, Allison dug out the protection and opened the package. She dangled it between her fingers. "Me or you?"

"I better do it."

She handed him the condom and watched as he rolled it in place. Jeff waved her over to him.

"Care to join me?" he asked as he scooted to the recliner's edge.

Allison needed no further invitation. She placed her hands on his shoulders and parted her legs as Jeff gently gripped her waist. He guided her over his shaft, and she easily slid down his erection until it was fully encased in her heated core.

Fire blazed in his eyes, "Let's get your legs over the armrests."

With her heart pounding in her chest and an urgent need to satisfy her desire, she nodded in agreement. With his help, she lifted first one leg then the other over the recliner's padded armrests.

Jeff carefully leaned back into the recliner. "Are you more comfortable now?"

"Yes," she managed to say, as an urgent need rampaged throughout her body.

Allison pulled in a ragged breath and began to slide up and down his shaft to meet his thrusts. Increasing the rhythm of each stroke pushed her desire to a higher level. She could feel the shudder along Jeff's shaft as his urgency mingled with her burning desire. With a quivering quake, Jeff climaxed, releasing pleasuring moans along with Allison's cries of fulfillment.

"I love you," she whispered in between pants of ecstasy.

"Me too."

She collapsed onto his chest, spent but happy. In the moonlight streaking through her sheer curtains, she could make out his features. His eyes had closed, and his hand traced lazy patterns across her back.

Finally, Allison uttered, "Maybe I should close the drapes.

Anyone can look in from the parking area and see us. Lucky thing we never turned on any lights."

"Honey, I'd love to stay and try out other locations in your apartment, but I have to get ready for my trip tomorrow. I'll need to leave soon."

"Oh." Reality hit her full force. She knew their weekend would end but hated to see the love of her life go.

After a few minutes, Jeff helped ease her off him. Then he got up, scooped up his clothes, and asked, "Bathroom?"

She pointed out the location, and he strolled away. Allison donned a robe and made some coffee. He'd say goodbye, but it would only be for a little while. She hugged her arms to her body as a sensation of loss without him careened through her. Jeff had said he loved her. Actually, he hadn't said those exact words but had just agreed when she'd declared her love for him. She trusted him. He said he'd call.

After a loving goodbye and waving to Jeff from her apartment window, Allison inhaled deeply and savored the lingering aroma of his aftershave. She went to bed, deciding to shower in the morning so her night would be filled with Jeff's scent clinging to her body.

She prayed her dreams would be ones of fantasy, hope, and desire and that she'd awake full of contentment. Loving him and knowing he loved her would make their time apart easier to manage. She welcomed her day ahead, figuring that keeping busy would make the time fly by until he called.

And, he would call. He promised. He wasn't another Michael. She trusted Jeff and loved him. With joy filling her heart, she closed her eyes and waited for sleep to come.

Chapter Thirteen

Allison returned to the hustle and bustle of work and charged through her day with confidence and joy. She was in love. Jeff would call. Things would work out. The kids absent from the previous week returned. The parents offered little for reasons as to their time away from daycare, but she figured Mondays were hard for anyone to function.

The day went by quickly as the children regaled her with tales of their weekend adventures. Allison mentioned her day at the ball game and eating hot dogs and peanuts. One thing struck her as being odd. Joel told her about playing a game with Tanner the previous week, something about a new toy they'd shared. How could they have been together? Hadn't he been sick and Tanner away on vacation? But little ones sometimes confused people. Then again, kids and timelines didn't gel at this age. It could have been a game they'd played weeks ago.

Before leaving the center for the night, Allison grabbed the tie she'd had cleaned for Jeff. The one from their elevator adventure. The one that started her hormones raging and unleashed her innermost yearnings. She knew he wouldn't be in his office but figured she'd stop in, drop off the tie with a note, and then go home and wait for his call.

Allison tripped lightly onto Jeff's office floor, knowing that Maggie wouldn't still be there. The guard at the entrance in the lobby said one secretary always stayed late for last minute calls.

She greeted the woman at Maggie's desk and showed her visitor pass. "Hi. I'd like to leave something for Mr. Ryan."

The secretary replied, "Oh. He's not here. His office is locked. I don't think I could let you in there anyway. I've only been here a week."

"Yes, I know he's gone. Can I put it someplace else?"

The woman looked frustrated, surveying the surrounding area of closed doors as if searching for a spot. "Uh, how about the conference room?"

"Sure. Thanks. I'll leave a note for Mr. Ryan in there with this."

Allison held up the tie and noticed a blank then questioning look cross the secretary's face.

The woman shrugged and replied, "Fine with me. Tomorrow I'll tell Maggie it's in there."

"Thanks."

Allison walked into the room and turned on the lights. Placing the tie on the huge table to the left, she pondered over what she would write. She'd tell him about the tie tonight, so the note had to be something personal, straight from her heart. Maybe "I miss you. Love, Allison." Or maybe something more provocative like, "I remember your other ties, Miss Alley Cat."

Something caught her eye from the wall on the side of the door. Pictures. No. Drawings. Children's drawings. Strange things to see in a conference room. She took uneasy steps as she shuffled closer to the works of art. Tanner, Joel, Rachel, Austen, Debbie. All the pictures bore the names of her missing kids from last week's schedule at the center. The ones whose absences had made Jeff's time there easier.

Allison's heart plummeted to the pit of her stomach and broke into a million pieces. He'd used and betrayed her. Just like Michael, Jeff proved untrustworthy of her love. Tears blurred her eyes, and sobs threatened to escape from her lips. She sniffed back the moisture, hoping to exit the building and his life with some sense of dignity still intact. But first she'd write a note of goodbye. Allison wrote quickly and to the point.

She had to get away, leave town for a while to clear her head, and try to mend her crushed spirit. When she returned, her goal would be to find a new job. He'd manipulated the class sizes to win her challenge, got what he wanted that she so lovingly offered, and wouldn't think twice about refusing her funding request. The center would close.

On her way out of the conference room, she walked over to the secretary and asked, "I saw some pictures on the walls in there. Were there children here last week?"

The secretary looked up from her computer and mumbled, "Yeah. Mrs. Williams and Mrs. Ryan went crazy taking care of them. Are you done?"

"Oh, yes." Allison gave a sad smile. "I'm done."

The tears fell as she drove home and continued until she reached her apartment. She quickly washed and dried her face and organized her next step.

Allison placed a call to Rina and Tina's mother. Although Lisa Mercer sounded startled by Allison's request, she agreed to sub at the center. Next, Allison e-mailed all the parents and mentioned taking personal leave time and assured them of Mrs. Mercer's agreement to take over.

She had to call Aunt Abigail just to let her know she'd be out of town. Breathing a sigh of relief when the answering machine came on, Allison left a short message informing her aunt that she'd be taking an impromptu vacation. She would explain everything when she called again on Sunday. That would satisfy her only relative's mind as to her well-being.

Where should she go? She checked her savings and checking account records and realized that even if it strained her budget, she needed time away from memories. With a sad shrug, Allison knew they'd probably haunt her anyway. In the morning, she'd hop in her car and drive. Some destination would pop into her head once she left the area.

Allison turned down the ringer volume of her cell phone. She wouldn't answer it, no matter how many times he called.

If he called at all.

Jeff couldn't wait for his day to be over so he could talk to Allison. A vision of the sexy woman he loved kept popping into his head and propelled his hormones to streak through his body. He'd initiated her plans with a slight surprise twist during his week with her after getting an up-front dose of what daycare was all about. Knowing her rent would rise to an unrealistic number nudged him to act immediately for the center's sake.

He liked her ideas to improve the facility to better serve his employees. Impressed with her assessment of the program's faults and capabilities, he'd given his planning and finance divisions directives for implementing her changes while using his new building partnership idea.

Her plan for one larger central daycare center was brilliant. An empty building on his company's property could easily be converted to a center both parents and children would welcome. More staff would be hired and additional children taken care of, easing the quandary he now realized parents always suffered through when searching for quality care for their kids. Hell, he'd want the same for his. And Allison had showed him the way to accomplish it all.

Maggie was out for the day, so he'd left Glenn in charge of arranging further details. Faxing all the additional information Glenn would need, Jeff felt sure it would be a done quickly. Loving Allison and pleasing her were his utmost goals. And he wanted to move past her challenge to a more permanent relationship.

His last meeting would be over at five, and then he'd have dinner with three clients. He couldn't wait to return to his hotel room to rest and call her. Jeff decided to wait and tell her in person about his surprise. He wanted to witness her joy at hearing about his plans to finance a new and improved Ryan's Rugrats. Tonight he only wanted to tell her how much he missed her and loved her.

Had she thought about him during the day? She'd been on his mind, and he'd found himself smiling a few times while daydreaming of their time together. Her compassion and love for the kids and the center added to her many wonderful qualities. Allison was fun to be around and teased his every fantasy.

Damn. A stinging pain seared through the lower right side of his body. This time, it was more severe and almost burned. What the hell was going on?

"What happened? Where's Allison?" A bleary-eyed, groggy Jeff directed his questions at his mother and Maggie who were sitting in chairs near his hospital bed.

"Thank God, you're awake. You've had an emergency appendectomy. How are you feeling?" Elizabeth rushed out her words, and a concerned look masked her face.

Head still spinning, he asked, "Surgery? When? What day is this? And where's Allison?"

The women looked at each other.

Maggie offered, "It's Tuesday. You collapsed last night after dinner. Your appendix had already ruptured. The hospital called your mother, and she approved the surgery."

Jeff closed his eyes as dizziness threatened to churn his stomach. "I feel like hell. When can I leave here?"

"You're still running a fever. The doctor says you'll be here a few days. After that you need to relax another few days before you can travel," his mother offered.

"I assume I'm drugged up, but I don't think either of you has answered my question about Allison. I was supposed to call her last night. Does she know what happened?"

Silence permeated the room. Jeff blinked his eyes a few times and took in deep breaths in an effort to quell the nausea rumbling in the pit of his stomach.

"Jeffrey, Allison's gone. No one knows where she is."

Every muscle in his body tensed as he tried to focus on his mother's words. Allison. Gone. The more he willed his mind to concentrate, the more confused he became. A wave of exhaustion hit, and whatever drugs he'd had screamed for control of his body. Sleep. That's what his body needed, and the drugs pushed for it. Sleep now.

With a last ditch effort to stay awake, Jeff uttered, "I loved her." She had left because she didn't get what she wanted, just like Laura. Sleep finally overpowered him, and he slipped into unconsciousness.

When he woke up, his mother still sat by his side. He needed to clear his head and get some answers.

"Allison's gone. Left without a word. She didn't get what she wanted, so she dropped out of my life. Just like Laura." He searched his mother's face. "No one knows where she is?"

Elizabeth shifted in her seat as she looked at him. "No. I'm really sorry about all this." She lowered her gaze.

"It's not your fault. I-wait a minute. What are you sorry about?" Jeff's mind raced with scenarios of her previous attempts to meddle in his love life. Had she done something?

She raised her head and stared at him. "Uh, I...we only tried to help you win. We wanted you and Allison to have your weekend together."

Before Jeff could continue interrogating his mother, his doctor walked in and spent a few minutes talking about Jeff's surgery. Every time Jeff asked to be released, the doctor shook his head and mentioned how dangerous it would be for him to check out of the hospital too soon.

After the doctor left, Jeff turned his full attention to his mother. With his patience worn thin, he demanded, "What the hell did you do?"

"I'll excuse your swear word because you're sick and angry.

Honestly though, you're an absolute horror as a patient. That nice doctor only wants what's best for you and—"

Utilizing his last thread of patience, Jeff interrupted her. "Please stop and answer my question. What did you do?"

Elizabeth heaved a sigh. "Maggie and I had some of the children come to the boardroom so you'd have smaller groups to work with. After seeing how tired you were, we were afraid you'd give up and never get to know that lovely girl. Abigail said—"

"Abigail? Allison's aunt? You got her involved in this too?" A major headache formed at his temples.

"We, uh, called her to ask questions about Allison's plans, and she was more than happy to help with the children. The parents were thrilled to be working on a special project and to give their input for a new center."

Jeff shook his head. "I don't believe this. You and Maggie and Abigail meddled in our lives? Didn't you think I'd find out? Or Allison? Shit. I wonder if she knows and thinks I was behind all this." Wheels started spinning in his head as Jeff created what-if scenes about the whole mess. Had this led to Allison's decision to disappear?

Maggie stood by the opened door to his room and eyed Jeff with caution. "Is it safe for me to come in? From the look of murder in your eyes, I'm guessing your mother told you how we tried to help."

His groan had nothing to do with physical pain. "Oh, Lord. Help? You two—no, you three—have done it to me again. But this time, I've lost the woman I love. Where the hell is she?"

Elizabeth glanced at Maggie. "He keeps swearing. That's a bad sign."

Maggie nodded and said, "I think we deserve it this time, though." She looked at Jeff. "We just found out that you had Glenn working on new plans for the center almost immediately. He kept quiet about your ideas, since you wanted it to be a surprise. It would have been so much easier if you had told us.

Maybe we could have—"

"I have to keep interrupting you both. No. Maybe you should leave my life to me. I can take care of things." He pounded his fists into his bed. "Do we know if Allison found out about the kids? How am I going to find her?"

Maggie's face reddened, and his mother lowered her gaze again.

"Mother? I'm waiting for answers again."

She looked up at him. "Allison went to your office to return your tie and saw the cute drawings the kids made that we hung in the conference room. So," she fidgeted in her chair, "I guess she knows the kids were there and thinks you arranged it."

"Shit." Brain fog began to cloud his mind as more drugs started to kick in, draining his energy. Jeff rubbed his temples, trying to soothe his headache. "All right, you two. Listen carefully. Talk to her aunt. Allison wouldn't just leave and not let her know where she was going."

He glared at them. "I expect some type of report before I hire a private detective to find her. I will not, I repeat, not, lose the woman I love."

Elizabeth stood and grabbed Maggie's hand. "We'll call Abigail. You rest. I'll call her from the waiting room. Get some sleep."

She dragged Maggie out the door with her before Jeff could respond. His eyelids fluttered, and he knew sleep would overpower his resolve to remain awake. His last conscious thought was of Allison, alone somewhere and thinking he didn't care.

"Jeff? Are you awake?" Elizabeth asked.

Maggie and his mother smiled as he opened his eyes.

"Did you find her? Consider yourself lucky I don't disown you and fire Maggie after what you've done."

His mother made sniffing sounds. "We've apologized a million times already."

Contrite, he answered with a sigh, "All right. All right. I

won't disown you or get rid of Aunt Mags. But no more stunts. Understood?"

"Yes, dear. Maggie and I talked to Abigail."

"And?"

"Allison is supposed to call her on Sunday. I explained how Allison found out about the kids and your surgery. She's upset since she helped us manipulate things."

Jeff smirked. "You're a definite meddling threesome."

Elizabeth continued, "She wants to talk to us when we return to straighten this out. Your plans for the center have delighted her. Abigail figures Allison will understand and forgive us."

Jeff ordered, "Maggie, make arrangements for us to meet with her on Sunday."

"Okay."

"Tell her I love Allison. She loves me, or at least she did until you two entered the picture and hatched your plan." He surveyed the room. "Where's my laptop and cell phone?"

Elizabeth said, "We'll get you settled into our hotel tomorrow. After three or four days, we'll fly you back home. We're making all the arrangements."

"Good. That'll keep you busy. Make it three days. I won't stay here any longer than that. I've got to get back."

Maggie handed him his phone and laptop. "Here. Your phone's charged, and your laptop's ready to use. I talked to Glenn while you were sleeping, and everything's going as planned."

Jeff turned on his computer. "I need to send some messages. I don't care if we pay quadruple time and have people working around the clock. I want that new center completed by the end of next week. I'll be back by then. Hopefully on Sunday, we'll find out where Allison is."

His phone rang, and Jeff answered. Glenn updated him on his new project. "Yes," Jeff said, "that's what I want done. And I want it done yesterday."

Jeff continued talking as Maggie left the room and Elizabeth organized paperwork he'd received via a courier.

On Sunday, Allison walked through Arlington National Cemetery, searching for her parents' graves. The day was quiet, the setting serene. She found their markers and bowed her head in prayer.

Aloud, she said, "I made a fool of myself. He used me, and I went willingly because I love him. Can you believe that? I still love him. How stupid am I? What should I do?"

She looked around and wondered if moving back to the area, near their graves, would be an answer. Would it be like coming home? As a child in a military family, she'd always moved every few years, never staying in one place long enough to make it feel like home. The only place she'd lived in longer than four years was half the country away where her heart had shattered.

Even as she considered it, she knew she couldn't move away from Aunt Abigail. And why should Jeff run her out of town? She'd find another job, maybe a teaching position. Or she could look for another daycare center to supervise.

Allison bowed her head again, saying a final goodbye to her parents. After doing some more sightseeing, she'd leave. And she'd go home.

Nerves threatened to hinder his recovery as Jeff sat in Abigail Minnetti's living room with his mother and Aunt Mags. He'd insisted on being there when Allison called. He checked his watch for the hundredth time. When would she call?

Finally the phone rang. All Jeff could do was watch Abigail's reactions to whatever Allison said and listen to her aunt's responses.

"Hello," Abigail answered. "Allison, dear. Where are you?"

Abigail bit her lip and looked at Jeff. She listened to Allison and then said, "You have to come back. I need you to stop by the center."

After a few agonizing seconds, Jeff heard Abigail say, "I know you don't want to, honey, but you have to pick up your final paycheck, and it'll be at the center on Friday." She shook her head. "No, I won't mail it to you. Besides, the children miss you. You at least owe them a proper goodbye."

Abigail gave a thumb's up sign. "See you at the center on Friday."

She replaced the receiver in the cradle and then turned to Jeff. "Is that what you wanted?"

He nodded. "Is she okay? What did she say?"

Abigail gave him a quick smile. "She loves you, she hates you. Apparently her emotions are having a major battle." She waved a finger in his face. "You just better be worthy of my niece's love."

"I want to marry her, if she'll forget about all this. When she comes on Friday, you all know what to do."

Abigail asked, "And we'll be at the new center on Tuesday and Wednesday?"

"Yes. I want you to make sure everything's in place. You can do your interviews then."

"We'll need quite a few more people to staff it," Abigail mentioned.

Jeff concurred. "I know. Do what has to be done."

"Can I sound like a mother for a minute?" Elizabeth interrupted.

He focused on her. "As long as you don't tell me what to do, yes."

"Certainly not. I would like to suggest that we go home and rest. We have a busy week coming up, and one of us just had surgery." She smiled demurely.

Jeff closed his eyes as he took deep breaths. "I can't think of anything else at the moment. Fine. I'll take your suggestion." He stared at Abigail. "Mrs. Minetti—"

"Call me Aunt Abigail."

"Aunt Abigail, thank you for being so helpful. I love her. Please keep that in mind."

Jeff pivoted toward his mother. "How much did you tell Aunt Abigail?"

"Why, everything, dear."

With a gulp, he said, "Everything? The elevator, the carpet thing, the hotel?"

Elizabeth winked at Abigail as she grabbed her son's arm and pulled him toward the door. "Of course. Well, just the things we know about. I mean, our spies at the hotel—"

He stopped short, sliding his arm out of his mother's grasp. "You had spies at the hotel?"

Maggie interrupted. "I know people there. We had to make sure you two were having a good time after all the conniving we did to ensure you had your weekend."

"I hope you didn't have cameras taking our pictures. Tell me you didn't go that far."

"Of course not."

In a relieved but weary voice, Jeff muttered, "Thank God for that."

The two ladies bid Abigail goodbye, and Jeff followed after them. Elizabeth turned to him and stated, "By the way. I'd like to hear about those interesting ties you bought. The manager said they're very unique."

Jeff shook his head, sighed, and trudged after the two chattering women.

Chapter Fourteen

With a mental push to get her feet moving, Allison strode into the daycare center, eager to complete her visit. Saying goodbye to her kids would be difficult, but she'd bolstered her resolve all morning with promises of a brighter future ahead.

Inside, boxes were piled everywhere. Lisa came over to her as she entered.

"Oh, I'm so glad you're here. I have to leave, and no one could sub for me. Tina needs to see the allergist. Please stay for a few hours. I'll rush right back, I promise."

"I...that is...what's going on here?"

Lisa called out to her two daughters and headed for the door. "Just packing up some stuff. I've gotta run. Be back soon." She turned away and sailed out the door.

Allison looked around the room and found Robert, Alex, Connor, and Amy busy putting toys very carefully in boxes. She walked over to them.

"Hi, guys. What are you doing?"

Amy smiled. "We're helping close up. Mommy said we won't be here anymore. Mr. Jeff said we could all help him."

At his name, Allison's heart skipped a beat, and she forgot to breathe for a second. Swallowing hard, she asked, "Mr. Jeff is here?"

Robert scooted over to her and gave her a hug. "I'm glad you're here. Mr. Jeff said you'd come. Where did you go?"

Confusion rampaged in her head. She gave a quick glance at the door and wondered if she should run before he appeared. But the kids all rushed over to her, surrounding her with their upturned faces and welcoming hugs.

"I, well, I went on a trip. Where's Mr. Jeff?"

"He's in the kitchen with Susan," Alex answered before he returned to a box and began dropping some trucks inside it.

Stiffening her spine, Allison stood ramrod straight and marched into the kitchen. She found Jeff on the floor with his head lodged inside the baking cabinet. Susan collected the supplies he handed out.

"Sweetie, take this box and put it on the counter."

Susan turned and saw Allison standing by the doorway. "Miss Allison! You're here!"

In his haste to get up, Jeff knocked his head on the cabinet door with a loud cracking sound. He sat on the floor, hand on head, and peered up at Allison.

"Susan, honey, would you go inside and help the others? I need to speak to Mr. Jeff." Allison folded her arms in front of her, tapping one foot on the linoleum floor with what she hoped was murder in her eyes aimed directly at him.

The child skipped out of the room as Jeff gingerly got to his feet.

"What's going on here?" She wanted answers, and she wanted them immediately.

"What does it look like? We're packing up. Where have you been?"

The man had the nerve to stand there asking her questions while bleeding. "Oh, for Pete's sake. Go sit over by the table. Your head's bleeding."

Jeff did as told, and she grabbed some ice from the freezer and placed it in a cloth. With an ungentle plop, she placed the cold pack on his head.

"Ouch! Thanks, I guess. Boy, you're mean when you're angry. But also gorgeous." He smiled at her.

"Oh, no you don't. Don't try that Randy Ryan charm on

me." Allison looked around the room. "I don't understand. I paid this month's rent. Why's the center closing?" She lowered her shoulders while making a fruitless attempt to stop the tears welling in her eyes.

"How about another challenge with a consequence, and I'll tell you?"

Allison thought seriously about taking his ice pack and whacking it onto his head again. "Absolutely not. I trusted you, and you used me. You arranged all those absences during your week at the center."

"Not me. I never used you. You can blame my mother and Maggie for that. What we had was special. Still is if you love me. I swear I didn't betray your trust."

She frowned, trying to sort through his comments although they didn't make any sense. If she still loved him? "What? I don't understand."

Jeff got up and moved to her side before gently lowering her onto a kitchen chair. "Honey, they arranged for the kids to be absent. Even enticed your poor aunt into their sneaky plan. Ask them. I had nothing to do with it. They wanted us to have our weekend and were afraid I'd never make it through the week with too many kids to handle."

Tears still blurred her eyes and threatened to spill over. She slumped back against the chair. "They did that? You didn't know?"

"No. After being with me all that time, did you really think I'd do something so underhanded to the woman I love?"

Still in shock, Allison stated "But—but you didn't call. I waited and—"

Jeff pulled her up into his arms and embraced her in a massive hug. "Remember all those annoying pains I kept having in my side? Turns out it was appendicitis. I had surgery on my first night in St. Louis."

Mixed emotions flooded her body. Love, care, and desire pushed aside anger and sadness. "Oh, Jeff. I didn't know. I'm so sorry. Are you okay?"

Tears dropped from her eyes, and he started kissing them as they fell. His lips trailed the tears to her mouth where he kissed her soundly.

Allison cuddled closer and then briefly drew back. "Am I hurting you?"

He cradled her head to his chest. "Not now that I know you're here. I've been so lost without you. I love you, Allison."

She stepped back and wiped away tears of joy. "I love you too. I have all along."

"You know, Miss Allison," he whispered, "it's my turn to issue a dare."

"I—what's going on here?"

Jeff responded, "We're packing up to move to the new center. You know the plans you had for your ideal facility? They've all been taken care of."

Allison blinked rapidly as she tried to comprehend what he'd divulged. A new center? He'd done that for her?

"Jeff, I have to know. Did you decide to do all this after our weekend?" Heat rushed up her face, and she knew a blush stained her cheeks.

He took her face in his hands and gave her an urgent kiss, one that screamed for more intimate moments. "I decided during my week with the rugrats. I had my finance and planning departments start work on the center, but I couldn't check on anything until that Monday before being rushed to the hospital. When I heard what my mother and Aunt Mags had done, I got everyone involved, even Aunt Abigail."

"My aunt?"

"Yep. And the kids and Lisa. Now, about my dare?"

"What is it?" She licked her lips, still swollen from his kisses.

"Marry me."

His smile melted her heart, meshing together all the broken pieces. "Hmm. I'll have to think about that." She grinned back at him. "And, what's the consequence if I don't?"

"Excuse me, but can we come in now?"

Allison turned to find Elizabeth, Maggie, Abigail, and Lisa standing by the kitchen door.

"Sure. We'll be leaving in a minute," Jeff announced. "I know you'll take care of everything here at this end. Allison and I will head over to the new center." He added one last comment. "I trust everything's set up?"

After a quick "yes" from the ladies and a few minutes of apologies, hellos, and good-byes, Jeff took Allison's hand and led her out of the building. Once outside, they headed toward Jeff's office so he could grab something he'd forgotten before going to the new daycare center. He pressed the up button for the elevator, and when it arrived, they stepped inside.

As the elevator started to move, Jeff pushed all the buttons, and it immediately stopped. He smiled at Allison with a devilish grin, opened a huge box sitting in the corner of the elevator, and took out a beautiful bouquet of flowers.

"Roses for the love of my life," he remarked as he handed them to her.

"Umm. They smell wonderful." She surveyed their surroundings. "The lighting's been repaired, and the air conditioner seems to be working."

Jeff removed his jacket. "Yep. Had this damned thing fixed last week, but this is a planned breakdown. I had the engineers rig the car to stop once we got in. We now have," he checked his watch, "fifty-eight minutes to occupy ourselves until we get rescued. And that'll only happen if I call on the elevator phone. Owning the building has its perks."

From the box, Jeff pulled out a fuzzy pink blanket and spread it on the floor.

Allison laughed. "So I'm a prisoner?"

"Yep. No escaping, so we may as well get comfortable. Care to sit down?"

They shucked their shoes, sat on the blanket, and leaned against the door.

"So. What's the consequence if I won't marry you?" Allison teased as she ran her foot up and down his leg.

"Say yes, or we'll be stuck here until you do."

He eased her down to lie flat on the blanket and positioned himself next to her. While lying on his side, he slipped his hand under her skirt and glided it up her thigh. She reached out and circled his zippered area with her hand.

"Allison, I need an answer and fast. Pretty soon I won't be able to speak."

"I'll marry you," she sighed as he bent his head toward hers. "But maybe you can arrange for this consequence every once in a while? I'm beginning to like elevator encounters."

"Think of all the great stories we'll have to tell our grandchildren."

As she pulled him closer, Allison added, "You mean when we turn an extra room in our house into an elevator and they start asking questions, Randy Ryan?"

With a smile, Jeff whispered, "Absolutely, Miss Alley Cat. Anything for the woman I love."

"How much time did you say we had left?"

When the day had started, she'd been desolate, but now she could only focus on the future. When his lips met hers, the promise of never-ending love mingled with the passion in his kisses. Allison knew she'd found her forever soul mate and the man of her dreams.

Acknowledgements

Breathless Press recognizes the following trademarks and names, which are property of their respective owners, used in this story.

Barney: Lyons Partnership, L.P. Rhenclid, Inc.

Honda: Honda Motor Co., Ltd.

Jacuzzi: Jacuzzi Inc. Corporation

Mercedes: Daimler AG Corporation

Royals: Kansas City Royals Baseball Corporation

Yankees: New York Yankees Partnership George M. Steinbrenner III, Harold Z. Steinbrenner and Stephen A. Swindal, all U.S. citizens, its General Partners

Author Biography

I've always loved reading, and began by obsessing over autobiographies and Shakespeare books. After adding romance books to my reading list, I decided to write.

Over the past ten years, I've published seven books: one nonfiction and six romance books. "Breaking the Cycle", a nonfiction, ghostwritten memoir of a speaker from a women's shelter, was published in 1999 as an ebook by Online Originals. My second nonfiction, ghostwritten memoir book about the life of a woman who lived in Sarajevo during the Bosnian War, is now available through Secret Cravings Publishing (their Living and Learning imprint)

Romance publishers include Jasmine Jade (both Ellora's Cave and Cerridwen Press/Blush imprints for Marianne Stephens and another pen name, April Ash) and Breathless Press (Marianne Stephens).

I live in the Midwest section of the US, and love the heartland area where I'm surrounded by lots of family and friends. I'm a member of Romance Writers of America, Mid-America Romance Authors, Published Authors Network, Published Authors Special Interest Chapter, Futuristic, Fantasy & Paranormal, Dunes and Dreams, Long Island Romance Writers, and The Author's Guild.

CPSIA information can be obtained at www.ICGtesting.com
Printed in the USA
LVOW041155290312

275218LV00001B/1/P

9 781771 010580